"Your opinion means nothing to me."

Jennet's voice was indifferent.

"Do you think I don't know that?" Rafe leaned over her, his harshly chiseled features bleak. "You hate me—and fear me—because I'm one of the few men who can see right through you to the mean little soul inside."

He meant every word, yet there was something else behind the controlled distaste, something just as potent.

"Yes," he continued savagely as he sat down beside her on the lounger. "There's lust, too—and you feel it just as I do."

"No," she protested, even while her body melted.

Only this man, she thought bemusedly. It had never been like this with Derek, not with anyone.

What was between them was love. Passion and hatred and suspicion— and love. She should have realized it sooner.

ROBYN DONALD, her husband and their two children make their home in the far north of New Zealand where they indulge their love for outdoor life in general and sailing in particular. She keeps a file of clippings, photographs and a diary that she confides, "is useful in my work as well as for settling family arguments!"

Books by Robyn Donald

HARLEQUIN PRESENTS

HARLEQUIN ROMANCE

These books may be available at your local bookseller.

Don't miss any of our special offers. Write to us at the following address for information on our newest releases.

Harlequin Reader Service
901 Fuhrmann Blvd., P.O. Box 1397, Buffalo, NY 14240
Canadian address: P.O. Box 603,
Fort Erie, Ont. L2A 5X3

ROBYN DONALD

captives of the past

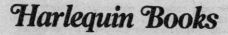

Harlequin Books

TORONTO • NEW YORK • LONDON
AMSTERDAM • PARIS • SYDNEY • HAMBURG
STOCKHOLM • ATHENS • TOKYO • MILAN

Harlequin Presents first edition February 1987
ISBN 0-373-10952-0

Original hardcover edition published in 1986
by Mills & Boon Limited

CHAPTER ONE

THE nausea which had been clawing at Jennet Scarth's stomach for the past week became suddenly acute. Swallowing hard she closed great, green eyes to blot out the sight of the big house as the taxi swung around the last sweeping curve of the drive. Stone walls glimmered pale against the dark hills behind, tall curtained windows were arched rectangles of golden light in the symmetrical, italiannate façade.

'Looks as though the party's in full swung,' the taxi driver observed, her voice slightly envious. 'Pity the bus had a breakdown, but you won't have missed much. I've heard that when the Hollingworths give a party most people stay on 'til breakfast.'

Her curiosity was patent. Visitors to Te Puriri Station in the northern province of New Zealand did not normally arrive by by bus. Nothing so mundane. Expensive cars were the more usual mode of transport, or the twice daily plane from Auckland. Some even flew their own light aircraft to land on the grass strip in the hills behind the homestead.

But tonight's plane had been booked up, and although she could have spent the night in a hotel in Auckland and flown up the next morning Jennet had chosen to take the bus. If she had put off coming, she might just have turned tail and fled back across the Tasman Sea to the safety of Australia.

She smiled stiffly as she paid the driver, then stood, suitcase in hand, her eyes fixed bleakly on the red glow of the tail lights, until they were swallowed behind one of the banks of shrubs, which were such a feature of the garden.

Tomorrow it would be all round the district that Jennet Scarth had finally come back to the valley. The woman who drove the taxi was a gossipy creature, she would not keep quiet about her fare, and once she had described her it wouldn't take long for someone to realise who she was. In Takapo Valley memories were long and she had left in a blaze of the kind of publicity which needed only a slight fanning to flame up again.

Jennet's pale hair gleamed like a halo around her small face as she turned, the lights by the doors colouring the shadows to a hue so close to pink that reporters always described her as a strawberry blonde. Now she shifted her suitcase to the other hand, lifted her chin in a small deliberate gesture and turned away from the big panelled doors to walk swiftly past the graceful windows of the façade. Gravel made small crunching noises beneath her feet. She shivered, for the air struck chill after that of Sydney. In Australia spring had already come; here, although the pure air was heavy with the scent of spring flowers, it was still the last month of winter.

If only the wretched bus hadn't decided to break down she would have arrived here before the party. There was no way she was going to walk in through the front door to face the avid speculative stares of Rafe's friends.

At least, she thought with a wryness which was her only defence against fear, with people around, Rafe was not so likely to use that bitter caustic tongue of his on her. Then she smiled, for she was fooling herself. If Rafe wanted to he'd tear strips off her in front of the Queen, and tonight he was going to feel just like that. He would take no more than a second to work out her reason for returning. And he would be totally, blackly, furious.

The tension in her stomach intensified into an actual physical sensation. Just as her quick steps took her around the corner of the building she heard the doors open behind her. Instantly she froze. Melly's clear voice floated out, puzzled and excited.

'I was sure I heard an engine ... oh well, too much champagne, I suppose.'

A man's voice—not Rafe's—said something indist-inguishable and there was a mingling of laughter which was immediately extinguished by the heavy sound of the closing doors. Jennet's skin was suddenly clammy, the palms of her hands wet. Her fingers trembled as she took the last few steps to the side door.

No light illuminated it, but by now her eyes were accustomed to the starlight and she had no difficulty finding the handle.

When it didn't move she was astounded. In the years she had called Te Puriri home, no door had ever been locked. But that was five years ago. Frowning, she felt absurdly like a burglar as she set the suitcase down on the step. Further on, around the next corner of the house, was the back door, but if she tried to get in that way someone was certain to see her. It led past the kitchen where Joy Webster, if she was still the housekeeper, would be busy.

Apart from two glowing windows this side of the house was dark. Mentally she counted off the rooms. The drawing room, then the first dark window would be the smaller room they called the boudoir because its graceful French furniture had made it essentially a feminine sitting-room. That left the next window, the one by the door, to be Rafe's office.

Stepping back, Jennet eyed its blank darkness. Surely they wouldn't have taken to locking the windows as well as the doors? It took only a few moments for her nervous fingers to discover its vulnerability.

Fortunately she was wearing pants cropped at the knee. Before she swung herself in over the sill she listened, aware that some small sound had been fretting at the edge of her consciousness.

Nothing impinged, however. Taking a deep breath she hoisted herself into the room's quiet emptiness, dropped to the floor then stood as motionless as a figurine. More than a few seconds passed before the unnecessarily loud thumping of her heart diminished enough for her to discern the distant subliminal beat of music coming through the walls and up from the floor. She stood motionless, staring into the heavy blackness with eyes stretched to their widest extent. Darkness pressed on to her with oppressive weight, making her uneasy, almost afraid.

It took an effort of will to force herself to remember the salient features of the office. Not that she had been in it often. Rafe had declared it out of bounds, even to Melly.

Surely the desk had faced the window. Stretching out her hands she took one tentative step, then others until she was brought up by a barrier. Her fingers trailed lightly over a stack of paper.

Yes, that must be the desk. It was, she recalled, an enormous Victorian piece of furniture, more like a table. If she followed it to its end she should be in line for the door. And beside the door there was a light switch.

Halfway in her slow progress across the room she halted, frozen into stillness like a small, hunted animal.

'Who's there?' she asked sharply, sure that she had sensed some slight movement.

There was no sound, no response at all and surely, if there had been anyone else in the room that swift, unexpected question would have been enough to force some betrayal of their presence, however slight.

Calm down, she adjured herself. She was not normally easily frightened, it was a perfectly reasonable tension which made her so edgy.

Trying hard to relax, skin so tight that she was uncomfortable, she took small, careful steps across the room, the carpet muffling any sound she might make.

It was, she recalled, an old Persian rug with exquisite mellow colours, a representation of a Paradise, or garden. Once her foot moved from its surface to the polished boards beneath it she would be close to the wall and she could grope her way to the light switch.

She was smiling when her hand touched something warm. Something that moved. Jennet's lips parted on a choked sobbing gasp. Her whole body stiffened as she swung around to flee.

A strong arm caught her across her breasts, a cruel hand over her mouth, stifling the involuntary scream which tore at her throat. Shaking with a sudden, useless fear she forgot all the precepts her instructor in self-defence had taught her as she was hauled back against a hard body. Her brainzed; it was purely instinct which brought her teeth together on the edge of the hand across her mouth, the same instinct which jerked her foot upwards and back in a sharp kick at her assailant's shins.

He swore, the short, crude words barely impinging until she recognised the voice. Then she sagged, swaying on legs too limp to hold her up.

The arm about her breasts tightened. He snarled, 'Keep quiet. Nobody will hear you if you scream,' and took his hand away from her mouth.

The sudden glare of the light caught her as she was dampening lips which were suddenly dry and sore. Her lashes dropped so that she did not see his face as he turned her towards him, but she heard the swift indrawn breath and then she was free.

She opened her eyes and smiled.

'Hullo, Rafe,' she murmured sweetly.

The dark, harshly outlined features were masklike. 'Jennet?' he sai said, the deep voice shaken. And then, more strongly, 'I might have known! What the hell are you doing climbing through the window like a bloody thief?'

'Well, the side door was locked. Why, Rafe? It never used to be.'

'Too many strangers around,' he returned impatiently. The black eyes hadn't left her face; they glittered with an icy brilliance she remembered too well. 'What are you doing here?' he demanded.

She covered a multitude of emotions with the slow seductive smile which had won her fame of a sort. 'Why shouldn't I be here? Why shouldn't I come to my sister's engagement party, even if no one saw fit to invite me?'

That superb, infuriating composure of his was firmly back in place now. He was regarding her with the cold dislike which had been his usual expression whenever he saw her.

'Half-sister,' he said laconically. 'Melly is your *half*-sister. And she's all Hollingworth, thank God. There's nothing of the mother you share in her. I'd have thought that there was every reason for you to keep away, as it's your ex-husband she's engaged to.'

'Don't be so old-fashioned.' Her voice was light, almost amused. 'It's two years since the divorce.'

'Four years since you left Derek—ran away with his cousin, at that. You learned how to humiliate in your cradle, didn't you?' His voice invested the words with harsh contempt. 'What brought you back?'

She didn't move. Not a muscle flexed, there was no variation of expression in her lovely face, yet something gave her away. His angular features hardened even further.

'I thought so,' he said savagely. 'You're too much Diana's daughter to be able to resist a chance to make trouble.'

Jennet was not an actress for nothing. Her laughter was unforced, without audible tension. Outrageously she fluttered long lashes at him.

'Oh, do be sensible, Rafe,' she said, automatically assuming the light, mocking tone which was a legacy from her first television role, that of a sophisticate, amoral and shallow.

That cool, amused voice had rapidly become one of her defences against those who failed to realise she was acting.

'What trouble could I possibly cause?' she asked with sly provocation.

'Oh, there are always buyers for your sort of wares,' he said deliberately, his eyes moving with lingering insolence over her face, cataloguing the smooth, pale skin, the faintly oriental slant of her incredible eyes, her soft promising mouth.

Reporters who stressed her strawberry blonde hair and desirable figure were accustomed to use words like exotic, or alluring, to describe Jennet Scarth. She was not, she knew, strictly beautiful, but experience, a lot of it unpleasant, had revealed that there was something about the arrangement of her features which attracted men. Most men, but particularly those who thought that because she was an actress she had no morals. They were always angry to discover that the slenderly voluptuous body and the promise of sleepy green eyes and smiling lips were not matched by an amorous disposition. Her armour was very necessary.

'I've no doubt you enjoyed saying that, but it's hardly an answer,' she pointed out. 'What trouble could I possibly cause, Rafe? Unless you think Derek is still in love with me, and that's not likely, is it?'

'Considering that you ran off with his cousin after eight months of marriage, no,' he returned evenly. 'As for trouble—well, any woman who looks like a houri and has no scruples is trouble personified.'

'Of course, all of the Hollingworths are as pure as the driven snow,' she replied, stung.

The hard line of his mouth widened in a humourless

smile. 'There are only two of us left,' he said. 'Melly and I. You are not, never have been, never will be a Hollingworth.'

The old refrain. How many times had she had that flung at her? Hundreds, probably, the first occasion long before she went to school. Rafe had always hated her as much as he hated Diana, the mother who had left her husband to marry Dougal Hollingworth. The woman from whom Jennet had inherited her face and body.

Glancing swiftly up she met his cold black stare with a gritty determination. He had eyes to drown in, so dark that his emotions were swallowed in their depths. Rafe Hollingworth, owner of Te Puriri and several other agricultural and horticultural enterprises. Rich, worldly, handsome; cold, cruel, heartless; stepbrother to Jennet Scarth.

'I may be everything you think me,' she said coolly, 'but I'm not stupid. You don't have to keep taunting me with being an outsider. You've always made it more than obvious how you feel about my mother and me. Your father forced you to be polite to Diana, but he didn't care how cruel you were to me.'

'Neither did Diana,' he said, hurting her with the same casual expertise she remembered from the past.

'Neither did Diana,' she agreed woodenly.

'Poor little Jen.' The words were a taunt, almost a curse. 'Perhaps if you hadn't been such a cold, scheming little devil you might have fooled some of us. Your mother was able to assume a surface warmth.'

Those long lashes fluttered down, hiding the pain that changed her eyes to stormy jade. 'I remember when I decided never to show my feelings again very vividly. It was when I was seven. My teacher had shown us how to make Christmas cards and I'd made one each for all of you. On the last day of school I carried them home, so excited. You'd been home from boarding school for a couple of weeks and Melly had just finished her first year at school. I couldn't wait to get home and give you my cards. I'd forgotten—or perhaps I didn't want to remember that every kid in that primary school spent the last day of school making Christmas cards.' Her smile was a masterpiece of restrained irony. 'Do you remember, Rafe?'

'No.'

She smiled again. 'It was the Christmas your father gave you his old rifle,' she reminded him.

'Hell, yes, I remember that.' His voice had an oddly soft, reminiscent quality.

'I thought you might.'

He reacted swiftly to the thin vein of sarcasm in the comment. 'What are you insinuating?'

'Nothing. It was easy enough to see that the rifle meant something very important to you.'

'Whereas your card didn't?'

She smiled again. 'Why should it? You had hated me for five years, ever since I arrived at Te Puriri. I can't really remember how you behaved.' Which was a lie. The little incident was engraved on her memory with a stark precision, just as if it had happened yesterday. Even the weather. The hot dry wind had torn through Melly's curls as the school bus set them down at the gate, snatched at their little summer dresses as they ran up the long drive, eager to give out their cards.

'Well, what happened?' Rafe's voice broke curtly into her reverie.

She shrugged. 'I was two years older than Melly so I got there first and handed out my offerings. You were all very kind. Your father told me I had done well. Then Melly arrived and I realised that you had all been waiting for her. Your voices, your faces, everything was different. I suppose I'd always known, but that was the first time that I'd ever faced the fact that whatever I did, whatever I was, I had no place at Te Puriri.'

'My heart bleeds for you,' he said sardonically.

Well, what had she expected? Sympathy? Hardly, not from Rafe. Yet that small incident had eaten into her soul.

'Was that the summer you wanted to go and stay with your father?' he asked.

She nodded, turning away. It had been stupid of her to reveal so much of herself to him, stupid and painful and dangerous. Rafe had an unerring eye for weaknesses. He could afford to as he didn't appear to have any himself. And she remembered from her childhood and the growing years that he had no inhibitions about attacking those weaknesses.

'He didn't want you, I remember,' he said now, unwittingly reinforcing her reading of his character.

'No, he didn't. Neither did his second wife. Naturally enough, I suppose. They'd had their first child a few months before. He was the apple of their eye. Naturally,' she repeated.

She felt his gaze on her averted face and just managed to avoid flinching because if she did that he would know how frightened she was and he must not know. Not now, not ever. But slowly, reluctantly, impelled by a will stronger than her own, her head was dragged around. Her gaze skimmed across shoulders as wide as a navvy's, up the brown length of his throat, past the severe strength of jaw and mouth and the arrogant line of nose until it was caught, imprisoned in the dark depths of his eyes.

'So you've come back to ruin this romance,' he said softly, dangerously. 'Do you hate Melly so much for belonging, Jennet?'

'I don't hate Melly at all.'

It was the truth. Years ago she had resented her half-sister in the bitter, all-encompassing fashion of childhood, but she was no longer a child.

'Then it's Derek——'

Her voice, fractionally higher than normal, inter-rupted. 'I don't hate him, either,' she said quickly, almost believing it.

'No?'

When she turned away, he caught her arm and pulled her to him, the long fingers of his other hand cupping her chin so that her face was open to his fierce scrutiny.

As before, he sensed the lie hidden in her heart. A swift hissing breath signalled his displeasure. His lips tightened.

'Like hell you don't,' he bit out. 'Well, you're not going to do it, Jennet. He knows you for what you are, now. We all do.'

Her pulses raced, then steadied. Against her skin his hand was warm and hard. She lifted her chin and his fingers fell away, but his other hand was still fastened on to her shoulder.

'And what is that?' she asked, half beneath her breath.

'A beautiful slut.'

The cruel words were spoken judicially as though he was a judge pronouncing sentence. Under their impact Jennet whitened, the fine bones beneath their softening layer of skin suddenly stark, her eyes desolate above a mouth which trembled before hardening into a line.

'You don't like to hear that.' He pretended surprise, but she read satisfaction in his eyes and knew that he was glad, that her pain fed something in him, some emotion she did not understand.

'I don't think any woman would enjoy hearing herself referred to in such terms,' she said softly, 'especially when they are unjustified.'

His handsome, cold face smiled. 'How sweetly you lie,' he remarked calmly. 'Your voice is as soft as a purr, low and husky and the lies sound like a man's most erotic fantasies. You're like your mother, Jennet, beautiful as a dream and rotten to the core. Go back to Sydney.'

'I will,' she said quietly, lifting her chin with a determination which was new to him. 'After I've seen Melly.'

'Why?'

'Because I have to.' She raised eyes suddenly clear and decisive. 'I don't want to hurt her, Rafe, but I must speak to her.'

Rafe was tall, a couple of inches over six feet. Jennet had always considered herself tall too, but his height was intimidating. He had a habit of rocking back on his heels and staring, heavy lids lowered over his eyes so that they looked like slivers of jet. He was doing it now, trying to read her mind, that narrowed, intent gaze searching the contours of her face, probing beneath the surface to test the thoughts in her brain. Always she had met that fierce regard with a wooden expression, deliberately concealing the shades of light and laughter which normally played across her features. The years had taught her that it was dangerous to let him see what she thought and felt. This time she ignored that instinctive reaction to meet the penetration of his eyes, her own clear and quite obstinate.

'Not bad,' he drawled after a tense few moments. 'Perhaps you chose the right outlet for your talents, such as they are. Or has Diana been giving you lessons?'

'Oh, you've not changed! You're just as cynical as you ever were.'

'I learned in a hard school. Remember, my mother had only been dead a few months when Dougal brought Diana home and by then she was pregnant.'

'Remember!' She flung the word at him like a weapon. 'How could I forget? A "friend" at boarding school told me, complete with juicy details, how your father met her at a party and seduced her away from her husband to live with him here.'

'It was the other way around. She seduced him.'

'Who knows?' She pulled away, still sickened by the memory of the other girl's ghoulish pleasure when she'd related the old scandal to her.

'*I* know,' he said harshly. 'I remember her when she first came to Te Puriri. She was only nineteen, just ten years older than I was, and I remember how she——' He stopped abruptly. 'Oh, forget it!' he finished, the harsh arrogantly-boned features suddenly wooden.

Jennet shrugged. 'I'd like to be able to, but according to Freud we carry the ghosts of our childhood with us wherever we go.' A little yawn was hastily covered. 'Lord, I'm tired. Is there a room I could bunk in, or have you a houseparty?'

He sent her a level, frowning look. 'Your old room is ready.'

'Is it?' She lifted her brows. 'I'm surprised it wasn't stripped and disinfected after I left.'

He surveyed her for a bleak moment, his expression impassive, the only hint of emotion the onyx glitter at the back of his eyes. 'I'll give you half an hour to get into more suitable clothes and then I'll come up and get you,' he said, daring her to object.

'No way. I'm exhausted and I'm quite prepared to let Melly have her hour of triumph.'

His eyes held hers. 'If I have to, I'll drag you out of bed,' he told her silkily.

'Walk into my bedroom, said the spider . . .' Jennet smiled, aware that he was only just restraining his temper. 'Don't bother,' she said over her shoulder as she left him, big and dark and dominating, his brows drawn together.

Once inside the bedroom which had been hers she leaned against the door, cold hand pressed hard against her throbbing heart.

'Oh *God*!' she whispered, shaking with reaction, her face white.

After a few minutes she straightened, breathing deeply and evenly, then slung the suitcase on to the narrow bed and unpacked it, moving gracefully around the small room. Nothing had changed. The green satin coverlet was still on the bed, the dainty furniture her mother had chosen for her in spite of her objections, the long curtains which hid the french windows. Even her books were still on the shelves. Sudden hot tears ached behind her eyes. She had hoped that one day she would have a daughter who would enjoy the same books. It was in this bed that she had lain the night before her wedding, so emotionally charged that she had been unable to sleep. It was this room she had longed for during the painful months of her marriage, longed for and known that she could never return to because Rafe wouldn't let her.

Well, it was over now. All of it. She had fled Takapo Valley and her husband of eight months and made a new life for herself, a satisfying life free from the entanglements and shadows of the old. And if Melly hadn't decided to marry Derek she would never have come back.

Lord, but she was tired! Since she had read her mother's malicious letter over a week ago, her sleep had been irregular, broken by nightmares and fragments of dreams. Yawning, she stowed the suitcase in the top of her wardrobe, then locked the door against Rafe and washed in the handbasin before removing all of her clothes and climbing into bed. She always slept naked.

Her last thought, before sleep claimed her was that he could hammer on the door until he was black in the face and tonight she wouldn't hear him.

Which made her shock at being ruthlessly shaken awake even greater.

'Get up, Jennet,' the deep voice commanded relentlessly. 'You've had your half-hour.'

Totally bewildered, she sat up, pushing her hair back

from her face. It wasn't until she saw Rafe's dark eyes rest on her breasts that she realised where she was. Then she grabbed for the sheet, covering herself but not before she had seen that red flare in his eyes and known it for what it was.

'You must be tired,' he said softly, and without exerting much pressure he put a hand on either side of her and pulled the sheet slowly past her breasts to hold it at her waist. He didn't look at the full curves he had uncovered; his eyes were on her face.

'Get out,' she ordered, but her throat and mouth were so dry that the words were silent and she had to swallow so that she could repeat them.

He took no notice. He did not even seem to have heard her. His broad shoulders cut out most of the light, but she could see enough of his face to make her shrink back on to the pillows. He looked—he looked as though any movement would crack the icy mask of control he wore. Tanned skin was stretched taut over the stark beautiful framework of his face. A flush scorched along the high cheekbones, his dark gaze devoured her as though he had hungered for it all of the years of her exile.

'So beautiful,' he stated through clenched teeth. 'Like every man's wildest fantasies in the flesh, promising unknown, untellable gratification of every appetite. How do you do it, Jennet? That hint of forbidden delights, erotic ecstasies, makes you a spiritual descendant of Helen of Troy, Cleopatra, Delilah.'

His hand slid across her cold skin to her breast. She flinched, but the hypnotic intensity of his gaze held her captive. An icy wave of sensation prickled over her skin; the warm slide of his fingers made her shiver.

No, she thought desperately.

She could not move. Like a statue of carved ivory she watched as his dark head bent, oh, so slowly, until his mouth burned against the curve of her breast.

Jennet drew a deep sobbing breath, held in a black enchantment like those nightmares when a nameless terror threatens and not a muscle of the dreamer's body will move.

'Rafe,' she whispered. His name sounded like an incantation, a spell, and she groaned it again as his mouth wreaked its own kind of magic on her skin.

He had never seemed bigger, more dangerous. Then, as if her voice had called him back from the brink, he straightened. Jennet watched the play of muscles beneath the fine silk of his shirt, a promise of power and domination. She was suffocated by his size, every instinct screaming her danger. Panic such as she had never felt, not even in the months of her marriage, drained the colour from her eyes.

He was no longer looking at her face. She flinched as his hand cupped the high, full curve of her breast.

'*No!*' she whispered, reacting violently to the bitter rejection which flamed in his face.

Swiftly she pushed him, her hands slipping over the muscles and sinews of his chest. For a moment he tensed on a predatory hunch, before the blindness faded from his eyes and he stood up, watching as with a shudder she hauled the sheet up to hide herself.

'Bitch,' he said bitterly. 'Beautiful, trouble-making little bitch. Sorry, Jennet, but I'm not as easily seduced as my father. Both you and Diana should have learned that lesson.'

'What do you—what are you talking about?'

He smiled, a savage, mirthless movement of the lips which had so mercilessly tormented her skin.

'Have you ever heard of Phaedra and Hippolytus?'

The reference was obscure. Jennet frowned, trying to track it down, her gaze held by the way her fingers pleated the soft cotton sheet.

'She was his stepmother,' Rafe supplied, and smiled again as he saw from her appalled expression that she had remembered.

'Yes,' he said smoothly, 'you've got it. She became enamoured of her stepson and when he rejected her she encouraged his father to kill him.

'I don't believe you,' she returned, her voice hoarse and shaken.

'Oh, come now,' he said brutally, 'after his heart attack my father wasn't much use to Diana. I gather she was always highly sexed and he lingered on for two years before his next attack killed him. Naturally she looked around for—company. I was the nearest.'

'You're lying,' Jennet said thinly, nausea gripping her stomach. 'Get out of here! You're hateful—loathsome . . .'

He laughed at that, irony grim as death in his voice. 'Jennet, you hate me because I know you for what you are, an amoral little bitch. If I'd wanted what you offered me when you were sixteen, you'd have jumped into my bed without a second thought.' He bent to run a scornful finger across her slender shoulder, stopping at her chin. 'Play your cards right and I might be more amenable this time,' he taunted.

She bit her lip, jerking away from the hateful familiarity of his touch. Against her back the pillow was cold and welcoming.

'I don't believe you,' she said hopelessly, because Rafe scorned to lie.

'Tough. I could have had her. Mother and daughter both,' he said softly, mercilessly watching her reaction from beneath those heavy lids.

'That's a foul thing to say!'

'It happens to be the truth,' he said, bored now, his expression shuttered.

He was angry with himself for using this weapon. Rafe was hard, but he possessed a strange kind of chivalry and this went against his code.

Oh, Diana, Jennet thought sickly, drawing her knees

up so that she could rest her head on them. Yet she was not surprised.

From above his voice reverberated in her ears. 'Get up,' he commanded. 'You're coming downstairs.'

CHAPTER TWO

'I'M tired,' she protested.

'My heart bleeds for you.' He was implacable. 'If you want me to dress you myself . . .'

She lifted her head, her eyes duelling with his. Neither gave way.

'Why do you want me to come down?'

'Because I want you to and on Te Puriri what I want, happens.'

Because she was tired, that was the reason. He wanted her off-balance when she met Melly and Derek. Well, he would soon learn that she had reserves of strength and courage well hidden from him. Her fragile appearance was no indication of her stamina.

'Very well,' she said cheerfully. 'I'll meet you down there in half an hour.'

'I'll wait.'

'I am *not* getting up with you in here.'

'One way or another,' he threatened smoothly, 'you're going to dress with me in this room. I know you too well. You'll find some place to hide.'

He loomed over the bed. Jennet said, 'How did you get in?'

'I have a master key.'

She nodded, then arrogantly commanded, 'Turn your back.'

'No,' he said softly. 'I might as well get some pleasure out of the evening.'

'Peeping Tom,' she flung at him before she threw the sheet back and got out on the opposite side of the bed. 'Voyeur!'

His taunting chuckle was her only answer, but she

felt his eyes on her body and it took all of her courage, all of her pride not to fumble as she pulled on tiny briefs and a half slip. There was nothing she could do about the heat which suffused her skin but her movements were steady and precise. Not once did she look in his direction. Every nerve shrank in her body, she felt raw with outrage, but she refused to acknowledge his presence.

Acting had made her an expert with make-up, and fast with it. Still silent, she switched on the lights above the dressing-table mirror, sat down and tidied her hair before her hands moved swiftly among the few bottles she had set out. It took her only a short time to emphasise her best points, her slanted green eyes and the soft bow of her mouth. After a quick, critical look. she added blusher then slipped loops of pink pearls into her earlobes.

Her hands stroked down the length of a drift of pale pink crêpe after she had pulled it over her head. Adjusting the elasticised neckline so that it revealed more of her smooth, lightly-tanned shoulders she said crisply, 'Pink sandals in the bottom of the wardrobe.'

While he got them she aligned the long cowl sleeves and pulled the waist into position, then checked to see that the slit in the gathered skirt was in exactly the right place.

Rafe dropped the high-heeled sandals at the foot of the bed. After a quick mist of *Ma Griffe* perfume Jennet bent, slid the sandals on to her narrow, beautiful feet and walked across the room and out of the door, turning towards the noise and laughter below with head held high and shoulders squared, her body swaying in the eternal female gait, sensual, an involuntary promise.

Just before she reached the bottom of the carved kauri staircase, she thought sardonically, I'm going to see Derek again and I couldn't care less. She supposed she should thank Rafe for such splendid detachment.

He had caught her up at the head of the stairs. At the bottom he slid an arm around her waist. Jennet stiffened.

He said into her ear, 'From the little I've seen of you on television you're a lousy actress, but tonight you're going to convince Melly and Derek that you wish them nothing but happiness.'

When she made no acknowledgment beyond averting her face, he continued, 'Or when it's over I'll visit your bedroom and take up that invitation you gave me seven years ago.'

The light from the chandelier glittered in her hair as she tilted her head, gazing up into his harsh, beautiful face through her lashes.

'If you do,' she promised, smiling at him with slow, practised allure, 'I'll make sure that you regret it until your last day on earth.' Her smile widened, she touched a slender forefinger to his hard mouth, meeting the sardonic appreciation of his glance with equanimity.

Like all parties at Te Puriri, this one was going well. The Hollingworths had a tradition of hospitality, an instinctive recognition of how to help their guests enjoy themselves, and this occasion was no exception. As Rafe opened the door into the big drawing-room the noise swelled out to meet them, laughter and much high-pitched chatter, a faint sound of music.

The first person she saw was Derek, his blond head bent protectively as he spoke to Melly. As they came in through the door he looked up, and although he obviously knew of Jennet's return he could not prevent the sudden fixed rigidity of his features. Melly followed the direction of his gaze. Her bottom lip quivered; she made a little hesitant movement before edging her way through the group nearest the door.

Rafe's fingers tightened unbearably at Jennet's waist. Conversation died away as avid faces swung from Melly and Derek to the two in the doorway. Jennet laughed and swooped on to her half-sister, arms outstretched and hugged her stiff, unresponsive form, hissing into her ear, 'Smile, dear heart. You look as if Banquo's ghost just bled all over your dress.'

Melly made a choking noise, half laugh, half gasp but her body relaxed and she managed to produce a smile. Jennet grinned at her, saw the anger and fear fade and released her with a final squeeze. Then she took a deep breath before she turned to face Derek, holding out both hands.

'You're looking well,' she told him in her sweet, warm voice, smiling up at him.

He took her hands, his expression well under control as he surveyed her face.

'So are you, Jen,' he said slowly, a glitter deep in the blue eyes.

Then Rafe draped his arm over her shoulders and Derek released her. There was a strained tense moment when no one said anything. Jennet's skin crawled. Acting had not prepared her for this sort of thing; unlike this one, most audiences were sympathetic.

She chucked and said mischievously, 'Well, now that everyone has seen that we aren't going to come to blows, I'd love a drink.'

'Champagne?' Rafe suggested in a voice as bland as it was deliberate.

'French?' She flirted with him from beneath her lashes.

He nodded, the hard lines of his face relaxing into that charming smile. To everyone who watched so eagerly it must have seemed that he was captivated by her. Jennet met the old condemnation in his eyes with composure.

'Oh, then I'd love some,' she said gaily.

As if she had given a signal those around them were recalled to their manners. Conversation began to hum again. Rafe tucked her against his side and they made a sort of royal progress across the beautiful room, greeting old friends, Rafe introducing her to those she did not know. After those first fascinating, shocked minutes everyone had grabbed at their social masks, their enjoyment given a keener edge because everyone knew that Jennet and Derek had once been married, everyone scented drama and intrigue and many were hoping furiously that it would blow up tonight.

Jennet sipped cautiously at the champagne, remembering that she had had no lunch or dinner that day, and precious little to eat for some days past. At the moment she was balanced on a knife-edge of emotion. Too much alcohol would tip her over, and that she could not afford.

It was like a nightmare, the big, beautiful room, the crowd of superbly-dressed guests, Melly with an emerald glowing on her finger, Derek watching from beneath his lashes. And Rafe, elegant for all his size, no emotions showing in the handsome face but those he wished revealed, Rafe who kept Jennet beside him as though she was something rare and precious which he had no intention of losing.

All the time eager eyes watched them, lips moved in fascinated conjecture, voices dropped as those few not in the know were regaled with details of the events of four years ago. And probably of that older scandal that had eventuated from Diana Scarth's arrival at Te Puriri as Dougal Hollingworth's mistress, too. Yet through it all the principal actors moved easily, with almost no signs of strain.

'Did I say you were a hopeless actress?' Rafe murmured as they made their way from one group to another. 'Sad that you can't produce this technique to order. You'd make a fortune.'

She ran her fingers up his arm in a parody of the flirtatious gesture. Beneath her fingers the muscles tensed.

'You too, darling,' she purred. 'A mavellous romantic lead you'd make. All that brooding passion, and you must be the best-looking man I've ever seen.'

Deliberately she raised her eyes then let them drift over him in an open assessment of his masculine attraction. He was incredibly attractive, with his arrogantly poised black head and his lean body, the grace of which belied his great strength.

Too forceful, of course. Rafe wore his character in his face, the strong bones and disturbing exciting eyes and mouth revealing both sensuality, and a strength which was based on total, bedrock self-assurance. And complete ruthlessness. He was the sexiest man she had ever met, fascinating in a dangerous way which drew every feminine eye.

His smile was a masterpiece of irony, while beneath thick dark lashes his eyes promised retribution. 'Don't mistake me for an actor,' he said softly so that only she could hear. 'I don't deal in fantasy.'

The chiselled angular features, so much more compelling than mere good looks, hardened as she laughed, the warm gaiety of it at variance with the quickly veiled apprehension in her eyes.

Much later Derek said cheerfully, 'Dance with me, Jen?' and without waiting for an answer swirled her off before Rafe could prevent it.

But Jennet's skin tightened and she knew that he was watching them. The dark impact of his gaze registered like a blow, wiping out the pain she had thought she would feel when she met the man who had been married to for so brief a time.

In fact, Derek's voice surprised her.

'What did you say?'

Anger thickened his voice. 'I asked why you'd come back?'

'Oh, come on, Derek. Whatever you are, I'd not realised that you were stupid!'

'You are,' he said softly. 'Otherwise you wouldn't have turned up. Your credibility is at an all-time low, Jen. Not that it was ever very high, was it? Rafe has always hated you and the rumours from across the Tasman of your affairs haven't exactly raised his opinion any. As for Melly—well, she's been in love with me since she was sixteen.'

Beneath the faint bluster in his voice there was unease, just as there had been when he had spoken to his cousin the night before Jennet had run away and left him. Then, as now, he was not sure how to deal with the situation.

Jennet's green eyes smiled mysteriously up at him. 'Has she?' she asked with a note of dry mockery edging the words.

'So she says,' he returned complacently, his good-looking face almost smug. 'And I believe her.'

'I wonder how long it will last.'

His hand tightened on hers; slowly he worked his fingers so that the joints above her palm were rolled painfully one against the other. It was a childish punishment, but effective.

'If you don't stop,' she said, 'I'll slap your face. Or kick your shins.'

'You wouldn't dare.'

'Keep hurting me and see,' she invited, smiling.

The inflexible note in her voice caught his attention. His grip loosened as he said warily, 'You're bluffing.'

'I wouldn't bank on it.'

There was a tense little silence and Jennet felt a surge of confidence. At last she appreciated her freedom. Derek was no longer a threat to her in any way. It should have been a moment of euphoria yet all she felt was a kind of aching emptiness, a sad pang of disillusion.

Suddenly Derek said, 'Got your eye on Rafe now, have you? Not a hope, sweetie. He likes his women

willing and we both know you've never been that, don't
we?'

'Do we?' she replied, with sweet malice. 'I've learnt a
lot since I left you, Derek. I don't think any man would
complain about my lack of willingness now. Not even
Rafe, but then, we all know he's an expert lover.'

As she expected he reacted to the implied comparison
with anger. 'So it was all my fault, I suppose,' he
sneered. 'Well, you'll have to pull out all the stops if
you want to get Rafe into your bed. He only goes for
the best, and judging from the way they fling themselves
at him he must be fairly jaded.'

Jennet laughed softly. 'Don't you think I could do it,
Derek?' she asked, touching the tip of her tongue to her
lower lip. Beneath her lashes her eyes gleamed,
mocking, seductive.

Derek couldn't drag his eyes away from her, the anger
in his expression fading to be replaced by a heated
awareness.

'You little slut,' he said thickly. 'Is that why you
came back? Are you sick of working? You must be mad
if you think you can get him to marry you. He's not like
his father, obsessed by a beautiful face and a ripe
body. Rafe's a loner. Women are a recreation for him.'

'Perhaps,' she said airily, deliberately letting her gaze
linger on the subject of their conversation.

He was smiling down at a thin, elegant woman some
years older than he. Charm radiated from him, not
obscuring the arrogant, bedrock dynamism of the man.

Jennet felt a tug at her senses and hurried into her
speech. 'But what I do is no longer any of your
business,' she pointed out.

'I can see that you might need money,' he said
consideringly. 'You got nothing from me, and Dougal
forgot you when it came to that trust, didn't he?
Certainly your greedy mother doesn't see it as her duty
to help keep the wolf from the door.'

Just listening to him no one would ever realise how furious he had been when he discovered that fact.

'So it's Rafe you want,' he went on. 'Well, good luck to you, Jen, although I'll tell you again you haven't got a hope. Apart from anything else, he's always hated you. Remember, he wouldn't even give you away when we were married.'

Oh yes, she recalled only too clearly Rafe's violent refusal to have anything to do with the wedding. He had, however, paid for it, something which Jennet hadn't known until Diana let it out a year or so ago. The knowledge humiliated her, for Dougal had left his wife extremely well off. It was symptomatic of Diana's attitude that she had assumed that Rafe would cover the costs of the elaborate, expensive ceremony she had insisted on.

'So if I were you I'd just head back to the soap operas,' Derek finished smugly. 'You really are not wanted here.'

'Well, that's a pity,' she returned, smiling cheerfully at an avidly interested neighbour, 'because I've just realised that I was right to come back.'

He knew what she meant. With blue eyes glaring at her he looked like some cornered animal, dangerous, every thinking process suspended in the instinct to attack. His chest rose and fell several times as he fought for control.

After some seconds he said remotely, 'Look, we can't talk here. If—if you're finding things difficult—well, I know I refused any support, but it's possible I was a little hasty. We could perhaps come to some arrangement.'

How like Derek to try bribery! As for refusing to support her, it was she who had considerably upset her lawyer by rejecting the alimony to which she was entitled. It was typical of Derek to forget that small fact, too. But she sensed that she could not throw away any advantage she had by flatly refusing to negotiate.

She allowed more time to pass before lying coolly, 'Well, things *are* a little tight for me now. I gather that Compton Downs must be profitable again.'

'It never was unprofitable,' he said quickly.

He lied. It had not taken her long to realise that one of the reasons why he had married her was because he thought she would bring a substantial dowry. It had been an appalling shock for him to realise that contrary to popular gossip, Dougal had not seen it necessary to leave her a share in the trust he had set up for Diana and Melly.

He emphasised, 'I never was in danger of selling up, but yes, things have improved.'

'Good,' she said, allowing a note of greed to creep into her voice.

'Not that I can afford to splash money around,' he said immediately.

'Well, of course not.'

Her eyelashes flirted with him. He was keeping a tight rein on his temper, but she could feel the resentful fury in him and was surprised that she was not afraid. During their short marriage she had lived in terror of his temper. Now she was completely in control, assessing just how much he had let his anger override his common sense. She knew how his mind worked. Even in eight months you can learn a lot about the most complex character if the incentive is strong enough. And hers had been strong, she thought wearily. One of the strongest in the world. Self-preservation.

Derek knew so little about her. His facile conclusion that she had come back to the Te Puriri to try a spot of blackmail was an indication of his lack of understanding. Like all self-centred people, he projected his own traits on to others, seeing only what he wished to. He knew that when she married him, she had resented Melly's place in the family. It would not occur to him that the years had given her the maturity to overcome this emotion left over from childhood's selfishness.

'I'll have to think about it,' she said at last.

'You do that.' He relaxed, conceited, once more sure of himself and his ability to read a situation. As he smiled down at her his satisfaction was patent. 'Just don't get greedy, Jen. Melly is very much in love, and I have a few other aces.'

Jennet lifted her lashes in a long, considering stare, allowing just the right amount of hesitation and surprise to appear in her expression.

The tape stopped then and she left him, threading her way between the dancers with quick, short steps, carefully keeping her face blank.

A hand on her shoulder made her stiffen. Rafe. Strange how she had always reacted to his touch, aware of his presence even when she could not see him.

Still without moving she turned her head to meet eyes which glittered like black quartz.

'Dance with me,' he ordered as the music began again.

With a sigh she moved into his embrace.

'Put your arms around my neck.'

His hands on her hips pulled her closer, moved slowly up until they were clasped about her waist. He met the quick rebellion in her glare with a flashing, wolfish grin.

'Please,' he mocked softly, and when she brought her hands up to rest on his shoulders, 'that's better.'

The music swelled sweetly about them, some husky-voiced singer bewailing a broken heart. Through the thin fabric of her dress, Rafe's hands were warmly possessive, She felt the play of muscles in his legs, the way her skirt whirled and then clung to the dark material of his trousers as they swayed together. Her breath came in short, shallow pants into her lungs. After a long tense moment, she had to swallow to ease

her dry throat. He was holding her firmly but not too
tight, and she swallowed again, unbearably stimulated.
Slowly, so slowly that she wasn't even aware of it, her
grip on his shoulders relaxed. Her hands slid down to
his chest. She edged closer, her legs barely moving as
she followed his lead. They were not really dancing, this
was an excuse for him to hold her, for her to melt
against him in a culturally sanctioned embrace.

The word he said beneath his breath reverberated
against her hands. She could just see over his shoulder,
but her eyes were glazed and fever bright, incapable of
focusing, the lids pressed heavily on to hot pupils.
Colour heated her skin. Almost wincing, she was
helpless beneath the sensations which were weakening
her limbs. They corroded away the armour she had
donned, eating at her self-control. Involuntarily her
body relaxed against him and she felt his harden in
response and knew that he, too, was in thrall to desire.

Thank heavens the room was dimly lit. What they were
experiencing was so close to the act of love that it was
almost indecent, she thought incoherently. She dared not
look at him. Beneath her hands his heart raced, a betrayal
blatant enough to fuel her own thudding pulses. She felt
the groan he gave as it forced its way from his chest and
his arms tightened, pulling her hard against his tense
body. For a moment they clung together like lovers at a
forbidden tryst desperately keeping the world at bay.

Then the song ended and slowly, reluctantly, he
loosed her.

All this time her gaze had been fixed at some point
over his shoulder. Now, still keeping her eyes averted,
she walked beside him to the edge of the room, her
hand clasped lightly in his, a smile fixed to lips which
felt swollen and tender. Savaged by a vicious
frustration, she had to ignore the insistent throbbing of
her nerves, the heated hunger in a body too long denied
fulfilment. She was terrified.

To hide it she flung herself into the role of extrovert, laughing, reminiscing, slyly flirting and all the time conscious of Rafe's dark presence beside her. For some reason of his own he met and matched her mood, the perfect host, the perfect escort—the perfect lover. Jennet discovered what it was like to be protected for it was only his presence which kept conjecture at bay.

Hours passed, and tiredness overwhelmed her like a black pall. Her high spirits became muted. Allowing the glittering persona of a minor celebrity to be replaced by restraint she spoke quietly and leaned against him, drawing on his masculine strength. Since they had danced together she had not once looked directly at him; her eyes had lifted only as far as the assured, half-sardonic line of his mouth.

Later she would have to rationalise that fierce frightening attraction, into nothingness. She had done it before, it could—*must*—be banished again. And with practise it had to become easier, she thought, irony revealing itself in her smile.

How old had she been, the first time she had been swamped by it? Thirteen, perhaps fourteen, a gawky adolescent puzzled by the rapid changes in her body and emotions, aware that her wistful craving for Rafe's affection had been replaced by another, intensely disturbing desire. She had not recognised it, of course, how could she have? She had watched him with puzzled, longing eyes all through the holidays. He had just turned twenty-one, magnificent in all the pride of his youth and virility, and he had been quite pleasant to Jennet. But it was Melly he laughed with and teased, Melly he loved.

After that she had not seen him for almost two years. Her holidays had been spent at the house in Auckland to which Diana had coaxed Dougal to move when Jennet had been only four; Rafe had been at Te Puriri, working like the devil to overcome years of neglect and the greed which had stripped the income from the station and left little to put back in.

Yet another black mark against Diana, in Rafe's book. But when Dougal had had the heart attacks which eventually killed him, it was to Te Puriri he had come to convalesce. So Jennet had arrived from boarding school to spend the summer holidays there.

She had not thought of those holidays for years, not until Rafe had so crudely recalled them to mind in her bedroom a few hours ago, and she was not going to think of them now.

Exhaustion made her stumble. Instantly Rafe's arm caught her, firmly gripping her. Across the room her eyes met Melly's angry, bitter gaze.

Very quietly Jennet said, 'I'm going to bed.'

He must have seen the weariness in her face for he nodded. 'Very well then.'

Somehow she summoned her smile. 'Sorry I've ruined your evening.'

'You couldn't ruin anything of mine.' His voice was bored.

'Nice to be so confident,' she returned, still smiling. 'Lucky Rafe.'

As well as Melly, someone else was staring. Derek. Jennet reached up, pulling Rafe's head down so that she could kiss his lean cheek. Surprisingly he didn't resist. Her lips lingered on the rough silk of his skin; he smelled very faintly of aftershave, but overriding it was the clean, masculine tang of his body scent.

'Good night,' she said, striving to control a suddenly shaking voice and turned and left the room, back straight, head held high, moving with a dancer's litheness, and only too aware that more than half of the guests watched her go from the corners of their eyes.

Although the homestead was centrally heated, the air in the hall was cool enough to bring a shiver to Jennet's skin. Set at too high a temperature, central heating would ruin the antiques with which the house was furnished, so it was kept just warm enough to hold at bay the chill dampness of the northern winter.

As the door swung closed behind her Jennet's eyes roved the hall. The grandfather clock ticked with sonorous deliberation. Te Puriri homestead had been decorated over the years with a mixture of antiques and good, modern furniture; it was welcoming and beautiful and just a little awe-inspiring. She loved it.

Beneath her hand the kauri bannister ran smooth and warm as she climbed the stairs. Bed had never been so desirable. Weariness was an ache in her bones, a deep lassitude which beat down the restraints in her mind. Memories came surging back like a dark flood.

Could one fall in love at sixteen? Of course not, yet the emotions she had felt then had been stronger, more potent than any since. Long days of summer had been a background for an explosion of feeling which made her tense even now. Because those holidays, Melly had spent much time with friends, there had been no one to squabble with, no one to take Jennet's mind off the king-sized crush she had developed for Rafe.

The pink dress whispered over her head. After she hung it up, she stared at herself in the mirror, her eyes moving from the high, full breasts to her narrow waist and thence to the slight roundness of her stomach. That summer she had longed for smaller breasts and a perfectly flat stomach like the models in the fashion magazines which Diana read; she had not then realised that it took rigorous dieting to keep those spare, photogenic figures.

She had yearned to attract Rafe's attention, to make him see her, just once, as she had seen him look at his girlfriend, with a kind of banked glitter in his eyes as though he was thinking unimaginable thoughts.

Ever since Jennet could remember there had been girls, even before maturity had given him that unmistakable air of virile magnetism. Rafe was used to easy conquests. That summer the girl in possession was his own age, a long-stemmed brunette who had seemed ultra-sophisticated to Jennet's eyes.

It was easy to smile now as she recalled how bitterly, agonisingly jealous she had been, but the emotions had been real and almost impossible for her to cope with. Unfortunately she had nowhere to go for help. She did not have the sort of relationship with her mother which would have made confiding in her possible. From her normal casual indifference, Diana had swung that summer to irritated condemnation. Nothing that Jennet did or said found favour.

So she had spent much of her time in a little dell she found along the valley. Each morning she packed herself lunch, her bathing suit and books and suntan lotion, before making her way through the paddocks to a small gully where totara trees surrounded a patch of lush grass, cutting her off from the working life of Te Puriri.

Time passed quickly as she read, and swam in a pool in the creek and sunbathed in the nude, feeling very advanced and rather wicked. She dreamed dreams, wove impossible fantasies for only two characters, her untutored mind playing with the concepts of love and passion.

So the days had drowsed by in a lazy procession until the day before she was due to go back to school. She had finished *War and Peace* and had dropped off into a light doze on the rug, her eyes covered by her arm.

A slight sound forced its way beneath the cloak of sleep. Rolling over she sighed, and then heard it again, fretting at the edge of consciousness. Slowly, reluctantly, she had opened her eyes, even then not expecting anything other than one of the numerous safe noises, the call of a bird or the snorting of one of the Hereford cattle just through the fence. When her eyes registered the tall figure standing in the shade of the totara trees she had gaped, frozen with shock as hinted horrors rushed swiftly to mind. Then he moved out into the sunlight and she saw that it was Rafe, his face totally impassive except for the leaping glittering shock of his eyes as they swept the length of her slender body.

The terror receded but she blushed scarlet and sat up, grabbing desperately for her clothes.

Quite calmly he asked, 'Who are you waiting for, Jennet?'

This brought her head up. 'No one!' she answered indignantly, hauling her bikini top on with infinitely more speed than skill. Tension and nerves led her to dropping the narrow piece of cloth which covered her hips so she made herself decent by snatching her damp towel around her waist.

Rafe came to a stop by the rug and stood with his hands on his hips, staring down at her. A sleepy little breeze carried the faint scent of horse; in her lowly position he loomed above like an old avenging deity from the days when the gods were cruel.

'No?' he said.

She could see his disbelief. Another painful flare of colour seared her skin. Her mouth set in a stubborn line.

'No,' she repeated stiffly, adding rather desperately, 'I come because—because it's quiet and no one yells at me.'

His dark brows drew together. 'So this is no lover's tryst.'

'Of course it's not. I think you're horrible.'

At the tremble in her voice his frown eased and he said unexpectedly, 'Yes, I suppose I am. Sorry. It's just that you're growing up.'

She stared down at her hands until the mist across her eyes blurred them. So he had noticed. She had to clear her throat before saying gruffly, 'Do you think you could tell my—Diana that?'

His withdrawal was abrupt and ominous, but even as she cursed herself for ruining the momentary accord between them he sat down on the rug beside her and observed, 'You haven't had much fun these holidays, have you?'

'I don't know what's got into—her,' she told him huskily, the words barely audible because she kept her head lowered and turned away. In spite of that defensive posture she could feel his closeness like a blast furnace heating her skin into painful awareness.

'Life can be complicated,' he agreed, 'especially at your age, but one of the reasons why your mother picks on you is because she is eighteen years older than you.'

This brought her head up. Frowning, she tried to make sense of the statement, her eyes suspicious as they scanned the dark determined face.

He showed his teeth in a not at all pleasant smile. 'You are very like her,' he said, 'just as she used to be. When Diana looks at you she sees all the years she'll never have again. It's all behind her; you have it in front of you. Diana's suffering from what is known as mid-life crisis; in other words, plain jealousy of a younger woman.'

His compliment shocked her as much as it surprised her. Accustomed to her mother's finished, polished sophistication, she had never seen much to admire in her own youthful features. The words stumbled from her tongue as she said so, and he had smiled ironically and touched her mouth with his finger, smoothing across the sensitive skin as though he liked the feel of it. A strange fluttering sensation in her stomach startled Jennet but she did not pull away.

'Of course,' he agreed gravely. 'But you are going to be every bit as lovely as Diana. Are you going to use this pretty face to capture yourself a nice rich husband?'

Her lashes flew up. 'My father is not rich——' she began in some indignation.

'No, but my father is. She's been married to him for a long time now, you know.'

Suddenly wary, Jennet turned her face away from the cold, taunting darkness of his gaze. She didn't know what to say. Until then she had accepted her mother's second marriage as a mere fact of life. She could remember no other situation. That brief, first marriage seemed not to have existed, and her own father was a distant figure. He had remarried and was not interested in her, his new family had all his love.

At school she had been teased about the scandal of Melly's birth and the marriage which had happened too late, but she had stubbornly ignored those who had tried to use it to torment her, refusing to care about events which happened so long ago. Recently however she had found herself wondering what there was about Dougal Hollingworth which had led her mother to fly in the face of convention.

Was Rafe right, telling her that it was money, greed?

'You're just being beastly,' she muttered, wishing that he would go away. Dreams were much more satisfactory than reality. In her fantasies, Rafe was tender and kind, he did not treat her with the rather contemptuous irony which was his normal attitude to her.

'Not really,' he said now, indifferently, pushing a hand on the ground to lever himself up.

Perversely, now that he was ready to go, she didn't want him to. Without preamble she blurted out a question which had been worrying at her.

'Rafe, is your father going to get better?'

'Diana doesn't think so,' he said quietly, settling back on to the rug.

He was watching her, his eyes half closed against the hard brilliance of the sunlight. The sweetish scent of crushed grass mingled with the moist dampness of the bush behind them. A dragonfly hung suspended, red and green, its wings a silver blur, then flew its short darting flight beyond the edge of vision.

Jennet sat still, unable to breathe, her eyes fixed imploringly on her stepbrother's hard handsome face.

'Did the doctor tell her that?' she asked, barely voicing the words.

Rafe's broad shoulders lifted in a shrug. 'God knows,' he said cynically. 'Diana doesn't bother to talk to me about my father. But you needn't worry. Even if he does die you'll not starve. She was the one who persuaded him into forcing me to buy Te Puriri.'

Jennet had not been told of this. The bitter anger in his tone made her shrink away from him.

'But it's yours,' she said, her high brow creasing with the effort to understand. 'At least, it's going to be yours when—if . . . How—why do you have to buy it?'

Looking back, Jennet could only think that his bitterness had been so great that he had to hurt someone. Dougal's condition made it impossible for Rafe to vent his anger on him, or on Diana, who would have had no compunction about complaining to her husband. In the light of his revelation that Diana had been propositioning him, Jennet could now only wonder at the strength of character which had kept him silent.

Then, however, he had lain back on to the rug, linking his hands beneath his neck as he closed his eyes. He looked very big, very forceful, in spite of the relaxed position.

'As you say, the station is—or was—my father's. After his first heart attack he decided to put it into a trust which would have given Diana a share in it for the rest of her life. So I decided to use a legacy from my mother's estate to buy the place outright. That way, you see, we're all happy. Diana gets a nice big lump sum to fritter away when my father dies and I have complete control of Te Puriri.'

'But—it's not fair that you should have to buy it,' she protested childishly. 'You belong here.'

He gave a bark of harsh laughter. 'Hell, what's fair? It was worth it, if only to keep her sticky fingers out of the till.'

'You really hate her, don't you?' she breathed, trying to overcome the ache in her throat.

He levered himself on to an elbow, looking up into her face with lazy insolence.

'Why should I love her? She's spent the last twelve years trying to cheat me of my birthright. You don't love her either.'

'I do,' she said, horrified. 'I do, she's my *mother*.'

'And I'm your brother, of a sort, but you don't love me, do you?'

A painful blush made her duck her head away from him again. 'You don't—you haven't——' she muttered, in an agony of embarrassment.

When he answered she could tell that he was smiling. 'No, I don't, and I haven't. When I look at you I see Diana, so I haven't set myself out to win your affection. Which is why you don't like me. But from the little I've seen of you with your mother, she's never tried either. To her you've been a nuisance just like me, a reminder that she chose a poor man for her first husband. Yet you think you love her.'

It hurt to have her inchoate, unexpressed thoughts put so bluntly, and she reacted blindly.

'You're just jealous,' she flashed.

He smiled into her flushed face, those impenetrable eyes scornful. 'Jealous? Hardly. Oh, perhaps at first. My mother had only been dead for three months when my father saw Diana. It wasn't long after that she was queening it here at Te Puriri. I was bitterly jealous then, especially when the first thing she did was to persuade him to send me away to boarding school. That was when I realised that she'd stop at nothing to get rid of anyone she saw as an obstacle. You'd better be careful.'

'Why?' The word was expelled on a shocked breath as she edged back away from him. He was too big, and that first electric awareness had been transformed into something which frightened and bewildered her.

'Because you're growing into a beautiful woman,' he said coolly.

Another wave of colour scorched her skin. Jennet bit her lip. She hated the way her body betrayed her, hated the sardonic amusement of Rafe's expression as those black eyes swept over her. Before she could say anything he added, 'God help the local boys when they set eyes on you.'

'Why?' she asked angrily, stiffening.

'Because any woman with a face like yours is trouble.'

He reached out and ran a long index finger up the sun-warmed skin of her arm, his eyes gleaming with an unknown emotion as she froze. Across her shoulder it went, stroking gently down the slender curve of her throat to stop for a tense second at the point where her bikini bra divided to cover her breasts.

'Beautiful trouble,' he said softly, some alien note in his deep voice sending a frisson of excitement through her veins.

CHAPTER THREE

JENNET didn't know what to do. Nothing, not her reading, nor her daydreams, had prepared her for this subtle assault. With dilated eyes and fast-throbbing pulse she waited, every sense fixed on the sensuous movement of his fingers as it delicately traced the outline of her bikini top. It was suddenly very hot. Tiny beads of sweat burst through her skin and she held her breath, wondering what she should do, and knowing that she wouldn't do anything because his touch, his presence, held her in a spell of lazy lethargy.

He wasn't looking at her, his gaze was bent on that slow exploration, but in the hollow of his throat a pulse beat erratically and she could see a soft sheen on his skin. Fascinated, Jennet watched as her breasts bloomed. They seemed to swell, to ache for a different touch; incredulously she saw the soft aureoles harden into tiny peaks which thrust against the thin material of her bikini.

Rafe froze. For a heartbeat the whole universe stilled. He made a thick sound deep in his throat, a kind of half groan. Then he sat up in one swift movement, his hands pressed into the rug, one on either side of her hips. Slowly, almost as if he was acting against his will, his head bent and his mouth touched the soft golden skin just where it swelled above the bikini top.

Lost in a black enchantment of the senses, Jennet made no protest, unless a harsh, expelled breath could be understood as one. Her dreams of lovemaking had been confined to kisses and chaste caresses. She did not understand this hot, unrestrained flood of sensation and was unable to control it. Like a woman drowning she went under, afraid, yet unable to save herself.

He said nothing, the only contact between them was the warm sweet movement of his mouth across her skin. Her dazed eyes took in the width of his shoulders, the cage his body formed with an arm each side of her, the red sparks struck by the sun in his dark hair. Heat crawled over her, slicking her body with moisture. Somewhere a cicada played his miniature zither, monotonous, persistent, so much a part of this northern summer that the sound barely impinged. The stream trickled leisurely over smooth brown rocks, the small sound cool in the heated, dazzling world he was making for her.

Every sense was stretched; sounds and smells lingered in her brain, yet she felt that they were completely separated from the rest of the universe, held prisoners in a golden sensual bubble beneath an unknown sun.

When his mouth reached its destination, the small peak at the centre of her breasts, she whimpered, assailed by an intense tightening deep within her, an aching need which jagged through her body like a shaft of lightning.

'You mustn't . . .' she whispered, not knowing what she said, impelled by an instinct of self-preservation which for a second of clarity overrode the sensual constraints of his caress.

He lifted his head so that he could see into her blind, hot face.

'Of course I can,' he said and smiled, a fierce predator's smile as he ran his hand up the tense length of her thigh beneath the towel to touch her. His fingers were not gentle and she flinched, jerking backwards, fear replacing the languour in her wide eyes.

'You're ready for me,' he taunted. 'Would I be the first, Jennet?'

Shame scalded her, shame and a bitter anger. 'Go to hell!' she snapped, trying to push him away.

Her fingers slid over the damp cotton of his shirt.

Before she could get any purchase on the hardness of his shoulders he moved, flipping her on to her back swiftly and heavily so that the impact drove the breath from her lungs and she gasped, staring up into a face set in lines of such harsh anger that she closed her eyes to shut him out.

'Yes, you'll be just like Diana,' he said, not trying to soften the contempt in his voice. Strong, implacable hands held her still as he bent his head and forced her mouth open in the sort of kiss she had only heard the other girls at school talk about.

Anger and humiliation lent strength to her struggles, but that relentless mouth held her in bondage. After a time she thought she was going to suffocate from its hot invasion. A small feral sound throbbed in her throat as tears squeezed beneath her flickering lashes. She went limp. His weight pressed her on to the rug, one arm holding her head imprisoned, the other down the length of her body, tugging the towel free before stroking the skin of her leg.

For a frantic moment she thought that he was going to hurt her, his body was so hard and heavy. His mouth lifted, and she took a deep breath, opening her eyes to tell him just what she thought of him. The words were never spoken. She caught a glimpse of a Rafe she had never seen before, the chiselled features drawn, the black gaze sightless yet aware, before his mouth came down again, kissing her eyelids closed, touching the contours of her face in a caress as gentle and seducing as that first kiss had been frightening.

His hand slid gently on to the nape of her neck. He whispered something she couldn't hear and slid his leg between hers, and in spite of her innocence she realised that he was not punishing her, that he wanted her as much as a man could.

To her astonished horror she was unable to prevent a leaping response. Her hand lifted, to touch with shy tentative fingers the smooth, hard curves of his shoulders, to slide beneath his arm and splay across his back. Without conscious design, her slender body stiffened in reply to the demand in his.

For a moment they were sealed together, mouth against mouth, the long sweep of breast and hip and thigh so joined that nothing could come between them. Rafe's big body was wracked with an intense shudder which called forth an answering movement from hers; she ached with a painful hunger in every cell, every nerve and her hips lifted and thrust in a spontaneous instinctive reaction.

He seemed locked into stasis, every muscle bulging with tension.

Then he muttered an imprecation and pushed her away, rolling over on to his side so that all she could see was his back, straining with the effort of his breathing as he took great gulps of air.

'Cover yourself,' he said savagely.

With trembling fingers, Jennet grabbed the towel and sat up, wrapping it cloak style around her shoulders so that it made a tent around her body.

Rafe got to his feet. She could feel the heat of his gaze on her bowed head as he stared down the length of his body to where she crouched at his feet, a turmoil of emotions and sensations clawing at her.

'Just like your mother,' he said flatly.

It was all Jennet could do not to cringe away from the fury she sensed in him. Anger rose within her like a red tide. He had humiliated her, deliberately and cold-bloodedly mocking her innocence with the invasion of his experience. She was torn by frustration, a new sensation to go with the others he had brought to life, the sweet urgency of desire and the bitter shame.

She took a deep, shivering breath. Although she was damp with sweat, her skin felt cold. It took all of her willpower to force her teeth to catch her bottom lip so that its stupid trembling would be stopped. Hot tears stung her eyes and her throat ached. The vibrato trill of a skylark seemed to pierce her eardrums, blocking out all other sounds.

I wish I could die, she thought desperately. If he says anything . . .

When he walked, he moved like a panther, silently as if his life depended on the successful stalking of prey, but she knew when he left. And knew that life would never again be the same.

Hours later, when she forced herself back to the homestead he had left for a dinner date with his current girlfriend. He was not at breakfast the next morning and immediately after that she had been packed back to boarding school, not to see him again until he came home from a trip overseas just three days before her wedding. And that had been two years later.

A kind of sob breaking harshly from her throat brought Jennet back to the present day. As if waking from a bad dream, she stared blankly around the room which had been hers on the holidays she had spent at Te Puriri.

It was incredible, but she had never before allowed herself to remember that incident. Frightened, repelled by such heated sensuality she had banished it from her mind into her subconscious, refusing to accept it and its implications.

Only a few months later her stepfather had died. After that, Melly and Diana used to spend the occasional holiday at Te Puriri, but on those occasions Jennet had always been sent to stay with her real father. Although she didn't enjoy herself she had gone without protest, as unwilling to face Rafe as he had been to see her.

Perhaps she should have made herself view things as objectively as she could. But at sixteen, who is objective? Even now it took all her willpower to think back to that time, to accept that something had happened to her in Rafe's arms, something which would have to be exorcised before she was able to get on with her life. By pretending those maddened minutes had never happened, she had failed in a necessary part of her growing up.

Perhaps that had been one of her reasons for her marriage. Rafe had gone to Brazil and she had been allowed back to Te Puriri. Derek had been there.

Even now she closed her eyes against the memories, turning her head into the pillow after she had switched off the lamp. It had been so wonderful, such a boost to her precarious self-confidence, to realise that Derek wanted her, that he thought her desirable and exciting enough to want to marry her. Inured to rejection, she found him irresistible. Diana had been very enthusiastic, very encouraging, turning what should have been a summer infatuation into a commitment. For almost the first time in her life Jennet felt valued, a person of worth. That summer she had bloomed.

It was this seductive feeling which had persuaded her into leaving university without a second thought. Even Rafe's icy, adamant refusal to give her away hadn't managed to burst the bubble of make-believe she had lived in. Because her father had been unable to come, an uncle had acted for him.

And then it had all fallen about her head and she had had no one to turn to, not Diana, who had followed her daughter's marriage with her own to a wealthy Englishman and gone with him to live in the south of France, not Rafe, who seemed to spend most of that year overseas. On the few occasions he was home, he had a selection of women with him and when he saw Jennet, which was rarely, he had made it quite obvious that he was not interested; couldn't care less about the girl fate had made his stepsister.

So she had relearned an old lesson, that she must rely

on herself, that for her there was no knight on a white charger to rescue her from the mess her life had become. With the courage of desperation, she had seized the first opportunity to flee, swearing never to come back, never to think of Te Puriri again.

Yet here she was, dragged back by the past, forced into a false position because she could not bear for Melly to go through the same experiences she had endured without at least a warning.

Above the ache in her head she heard the thick sound of a car door slamming. There was a burst of laughter, and other sounds that made it clear that the party was over.

It took twenty minutes for them all to go, but at last they did. Within a few moments the sound Jennet had been waiting for, a single sharp tap on the door, brought her upright in the bed. Rafe's voice said something which was lost as Melly flung the door open.

'. . . if she is asleep,' Melly finished, switching on the light with a ruthless hand. 'Go away, Rafe, I don't need you.'

Jennet watched, her mouth smiling, the expression in her eyes hidden by her lashes.

Melly bit her lip, revealing a combination of anger and pain. 'Please, Rafe,' she said again, and frowning, his gaze very hard as it rested on Jennet's lovely mocking face, he left them, closing the door behind him.

Melly stood rigidly, her hands very still by her sides.

'Oh, sit down,' Jennet said tiredly. 'It's me, remember, your sister, not Dracula.'

'Why did you come back?'

'I'm beginning to wonder.' Jennet affected a yawn. 'Believe me, had I known that I was going to cause so much trouble, I'd have stayed away. I've had Rafe threatening me with instant execution if I upset you, and Derek informing me that no matter what I tell you

you'll remain faithful because you're besotted with him.'

'Derek didn't say any such thing,' Melly flashed fiercely.

A strike home, Jennet thought with satisfaction. She patted the bed. 'Well, words to that effect. Come and sit down, let's get re-acquainted. It's been a long time.'

Melly stared at her. 'You really mean it,' she burst out, astonished. 'You know, you're really something! Tell me why you came back, please, Jennet.'

'To see you. You are, let's face it, all that I've got for a family.'

'You haven't cared much for us for the past five years and let's face something else, Jennet, you didn't have much time for any of us before that. You hated Rafe, and you used to stare right through me—you were a funny, cold creature, making sure that nobody got near enough to touch you.' She was sallow beneath her cosmetics except for a bright spot on each cheekbone. Her eyes, so like Rafe's, glittered angrily. 'You came back to stop me marrying Derek, didn't you?'

'Why should I want to do that? *I* left Derek, not the other way around.'

Her half-sister's long hands clenched again. 'Yes, you ran away with Trent—with another man. Ask yourself if any man would want you back after that. You're so pretty, Jen, can't you——?' She stopped to banish the note of pleading in her voice before saying woodenly, 'This is a mistake. I'll see you in the morning.'

So she wasn't as confident of her power over Derek as she wanted to seem. Jennet could have wept for her, so proud, so *young*, as she swung towards the door. Perhaps she was wrong to come back, perhaps . . .

Then she remembered the psychiatrist she had consulted. Ultimately her presence here would be kinder to Melly than her absence could ever be, even if she caused her some suffering. But it took hours before she was able to sleep, and she woke in the morning fretted by the helplessness which had driven her away from the valley.

Breakfast was served, as always, in the small room off the kitchen. Jennet was late, but not late enough to eat alone. As she opened the door she was met by two pairs of identical and inimical eyes.

'Good morning,' she said cheerfully, smiling as though it was a good morning.

Neither Melly nor Rafe returned the smile.

'Oh well, I tried,' Jennet told the cat as she sat down. She sighed and got to her feet again, to get cutlery and a napkin for herself.

'I thought you might sleep in,' Melly said defensively. 'Do you want some toast?'

'Just coffee, thanks.'

'You'd better eat something,' Rafe ordered. 'Or do you have to diet constantly?'

'Not yet.'

He lifted his brows, smiling unpleasantly. 'Of course, actresses are allowed a little more leeway than models, aren't they?'

'You should know,' Jennet said with cool composure. 'Wasn't your last lover a model? Of sorts?'

Melly gave a gasp, hastily smothered, then handed the coffee she had just poured across the table, her shocked eyes darting from Jennet's serene face to Rafe's.

He said calmly, 'Yes, she did some modelling, I believe, but as it was a favour for a friend she was no more a model than you are an actress.' His lashes lifted. Offensively he finished, 'She had the same decorative impact. Possibly with a little more style.'

Jennet grinned. 'What a nasty tongue you have,' she marvelled. 'Shall I tell you about my debut as Juliet?'

Melly stared. 'As in "Romeo and"?'

'Yes.' Jennet sipped her coffee, her mocking glance meeting Rafe's. 'I've just finished in it at Sydney.'

There was a moment's stretched silence before Melly asked stiffly, 'Good reviews?'

Jennet shrugged. 'Not too bad, although all with a distinct air of surprise.'

Rafe broke the subsequent silence. 'What are you planning to do today?' he asked, addressing the question in an indifferent voice to Jennet.

'I thought I might go across and see Derek.'

'How?'

Ignoring Melly's swift antagonism, Jennet suggested with a light lack of emphasis, 'Borrow a car?'

'I'll need to check your driving before I let you loose in one of my vehicles,' he said.

'Rafe, I've been driving for ten years.'

'Badly for the first three, at least.'

She knew that tone of voice. Implacable; Rafe was not going to take her word for anything. Firmly squelching the desire to fling the contents of her cup at his sardonic face she drank the coffee, slowly, silently, before getting to her feet.

Joy, the housekeeper, came in, They exchanged greetings and Joy refused Jennet's offer to help with her usual brusque off-handedness. When Jennet left the room Rafe followed.

'We're going into Port Arthur for lunch,' he informed her. 'Be ready in half an hour.'

'I don't——'

He halted her progress up the stairs by putting his hand over hers on the balustrade. The long fingers flexed, effectively trapping hers. Jennet bit her lip.

'Don't be a bore, Jennet.'

She met his arrogant glance defiantly. 'But——'

'Jennet.'

Her name was a warning, a threat delivered in two soft syllables.

'Oh, very well,' she retorted as the tiny hairs up her spine stiffened.

He smiled most unpleasantly and lifted his hand from hers. For a second she stood motionless, her face blank and smooth as she looked at him. He wore a checked shirt, the long sleeves rolled up above his elbows, and a pair of working trousers which hugged his slim hips, and those long. heavily-muscles legs. He could have been a farmhand, except that the clothes he wore were totally eclipsed by the man. He was dominant male, predatory, dangerous, watching her with an insolent amusement in the black depths of his eyes.

'Casting a spell, Jennet?'

The heavy pale tresses moved like a swathe of silk about her face and neck as she shook her head, slowly, just once. She was remembering how he had looked at her naked breasts the night before. All he had wanted to do was humiliate her, yet some instinct, feminine and as old as femininity, told her that his actions were based on more than the desire to punish.

'Rafe,' she said, 'Rafe, did Diana really want you?'

His first reaction was surprise but that was swiftly hidden. In a voice that was flat and cruel he answered, 'Yes she did.'

Jennet couldn't prevent a quick, shocked breath.

He smiled, taunting her. 'When I turned her down she had a discreet affair with—well, it doesn't matter who. He was too young to know better. Fortunately as soon as he found out, his father packed him off to Australia. She doesn't cope well with frustration, your mother.'

She couldn't bear the knowing note in his voice. Quickly, as if he contaminated her, she turned away.

Soft and deadly, his next statement stopped her. 'I wouldn't turn you down, Jennet, not as I did her. Last time you were a child. The same reason doesn't apply now.'

Jennet's skin crawled. It took self-control beyond anything she had ever needed to say drily, 'On short rations, Rafe? Can't you get what you crave?'

'I crave nothing.' His hand bit into her shoulder, swinging her around to face him. He was smiling again, that hard mirthless movement of his lips which meant that he was barely able to control his anger. As if she were for sale he swept her with an insolent glance.

'You're very desirable,' he said before leaning forward to whisper, 'and not in the least innocent. I'm going to see how well you decorate my bed before you leave here.'

A spear of sharp, hot desire ran through her body, but she stood her ground, resisting the sensation. It was galling to have to bite back the answer which burned on her tongue, but something in his arrogantly smiling face warned her that she had provoked him far enough. Too far, and he was quite capable of throwing her out of the house and refusing to allow her back.

'Then I hope you sleep in black satin sheets,' she said contemptuously. 'I've heard that I show up to best advantage on them.'

'Indeed? I remember how very tempting you looked on that old rug,' he returned caressingly, adding as the angry colour surged through her skin, 'but if you like satin sheets then I'll get Joy to buy some. Who am I to deny you your whims?'

'You needn't bother. If I did feel like cutting loose it wouldn't be with a man who can't distinguish between me and my mother. You make me feel sick.'

'No, I make you feel hungry,' he said mockingly.

Damn him, but he was right. For as long as she could remember he had affected her powerfully; it was as though he stripped a skin from her so that she was acutely sensitive, as open to influence as she had been when a child. He had only to look at her, even as he was now with anger and desire warring in his eyes, and she felt that tormenting ache begin to heat the pit of her stomach. Lust, pure and simple, just the primitive basic urge to mate, yet she had to clench her jaw to prevent herself from betraying it, forcibly jerk her mind from contemplating the erotic, tantalising images which formed there.

'As for your mother,' he said softly, watching her with eyes which saw everything, 'you're a fool if you think I can't tell the difference. She *is* eighteen years older than you.'

'That's not what I meant.'

'No, I suppose not.' He picked up her hand and drew it to his mouth, holding it so that when he spoke his lips just touched the soft palm. 'Very well, then, you look like her, you behave like her and as far as I can tell, you react to men in exactly the same way. Very generously.'

What would he say if she told him that he was the only man who had ever made her feel wanton? Refuse to believe her, of course. Totally cynical, it would never occur to him that even her precipitate flight from her marriage had been completely innocent. Trent Addison, Derek's cousin, was that rare person, a chivalrous man; he had made no attempt to touch her. He had just helped her to get away.

Since she had become well known, there had been gossip and rumours about her love life, but nothing was ever openly stated. Mainly because there was nothing to comment on. Her physical reactions seemed to have been frozen in some limbo.

At least they had been frozen—until she had returned to Te Puriri, and there it was, just as if she were sixteen again, palpitatingly conscious of only one man, the one man she couldn't have, because when he looked at her he saw Diana, the woman who had usurped his mother's place, banished him from Te Puriri and with her particular brand of callousness had made him an interloper, unwanted by his father, deprived of his heritage.

Rafe was clever, with a cold, logical brain, but the events of childhood can shadow the emotions of the man and he was unable to shake off his suspicion and resentment. Reason must tell him that just because she looked like Diana, Jennet was not necessarily her carbon copy.

Unfortunately there was a little more to fuel his antagonism than the uncanny resemblance and the emotions carried over from his childhood. There was that unfortunate incident when she had surrendered so completely to him, there was her marriage and her subsequent flight with another man, her appearance in the soap opera as an amoral bitch, her arrival back here and his realisation that she wanted to prevent Melly from marrying Derek.

'Generous? Perhaps,' she said indifferently, turning away to climb the stairs. 'But not to you, Rafe.'

His soft laughter was drowned by Melly's voice, low-pitched and angry as she came down the hall.

He made no reply to whatever she had said.

Jennet stopped. Over her shoulder she saw them both watching her.

'Rafe,' she said sweetly.

He lifted his brows.

'Do you think the end ever justifies the means?'

The dark brows drew together. 'No.'

'Oh, I do hope you're wrong,' Jennet replied, bestowing a warm, mischievous smile on them before she ran lightly up the rest of the stairs.

CHAPTER FOUR

HALF an hour later she came back downstairs, humming softly to herself. She had a warm, huskily sensual voice, not strong enough to be exploited, but very pleasant on the ear. Melly waited at the foot of the stairs, her face still and cold.

'*Chorus of the Hebrew Slaves*, by Verdi,' she said, and her voice softened. 'Do you remember the first time you heard that? Rafe played it one night and you demanded instant silence. We were so astonished that we all shut up. And at the end you burst into tears and ran up to your room. I remember Rafe wouldn't let me follow you. He said that you needed time to recover yourself. Do you still react so violently?'

'I manage to hide the tears,' Jennet told her drily, 'but yes, music gives me an emotional high. I read a lot, I love reading, but it's music and some poetry which really get to me.'

Her fingers smoothed lovingly over a small sculpture on a console, an Italian figurine of Cupid and Psyche, charming, sensual yet delicate. 'Somewhere I read that when Verdi died and the funeral cortege was going through the streets the passers-by began to sing that chorus, spontaneously, everyone just joining in. I hope it's true.'

Melly smiled, her eyes puzzled. 'You're a funny mixture. Sentimental yet tough.'

She lifted her hand in a little cut-off gesture to express her failure to understand. The emerald on her finger caught in the sunlight which spilled in through the door and the stone took fire, glittering with green flames. For a long moment both women stared at it.

Jennet's nail bit into her palms. Slowly she lifted her head to look imploringly at Melly. But Melly's black eyes were as inscrutable as any Oriental's, and the strong bones of her face were clenched. Jennet turned and walked out through the great panelled doors into the winter sunshine. Her heels tapped crisply down the marble steps and along the path, the sound ceasing as she paused to inspect a big jardiniere which held a camellia just coming into full bloom. The perfectly formal flowers were striped and flecked in two shades of pink.

'Helenore,' Jennet remembered, touching a flower with a pale fingernail. 'I wonder if I can still recall their names. I'm so glad your great-great-great, or whatever he was, grandfather decided to build himself a white villa instead of a sober Victorian homestead, even if everyone thought he was mad.'

Her gaze swept across the façade with its arched, beautifully proportioned windows.

Sheltered in its valley by the enormous old trees which gave the station its name, Te Puriri homestead was embowered by flowers, many of them in urns and pots which kept Ted, the housekeeper's husband, so busy. Now camellias were arranged along the path; sharing their urns were violets and ivy and tiny cream and white narcissi. Across the lawns in borders, beneath magnolia and jacaranda trees, were other narcissi, jonquils like small suns and above them daphne bushes, the clean spicy scent of the little rosy flowers mingling with the perfume of the jonquils. Japonica and poinsettia provided colour and form, the one spikily elegant, the other lending the garden a touch of tropical colour. Clumps of polyanthus made a Persian carpet, and at a focal point down the drive a huge Taiwan cherry tree was smothered in its tiny cerise bells, the delight of every tui from miles around. The abrupt, tearing sound of their flight almost drowned out the clucks and chirps and exquisite chimes of their song.

'You really do love the place, don't you?'

Jennet suppressed a start at Melly's soft statement. She turned a dazzled face over her shoulder and met the impact of two pairs of black eyes. Rafe had joined his half-sister and was watching, his expression guarded.

'I've always loved it,' Jennet shrugged. 'I used to believe that it was the most beautiful place in the world.'

She reacted to Rafe's cold stare with the sparkling smile she used to hide her emotions. He frowned, the sunlight highlighting strong cheekbones and the autocratic line of his jaw, his eyes sweeping her in a scrutiny as intense as it was bleak.

She knew she looked good. Her tapered, pleated pants in grey silk boucle emphasised the long feminine legs and narrow ankles. With them, she wore high suede shoes of the same grey and a striped print shirt, keeping the cool wind at bay with a grey linen blazer. Just a little too formally dressed for a shopping trip in a small country town, she was, beside Rafe and Melly's splendid, natural throwaway grace, perhaps too finished, a little artificial, but she could not compete with their tall balanced bodies and striking bone structure. She needed the armour that good clothes provided.

Port Arthur had slept away most of the years since before the end of the last century when the last kauri had been felled, until ten years ago when tourists had begun to appreciate its air of dreaming peace.

The locals woke up to find themselves living in a holiday centre; many of them disliked the change but quite a few were far-sighted enough to see the opportunities this offered. Rafe had been one. As well as an excellent landowner, he was an astute businessman and had bought into the development of the little port.

What an unfair decision Dougal had made when he had forced Rafe to buy the station. No wonder Rafe despised the stepmother who had persuaded his father to make it. It was just unfortunate that he wasn't entirely rational where Diana's daughter was concerned.

Not for the first time, Jennet wondered how he would respond if she told him the reason why she had fled her marriage. As her eyes roamed the familiar contours of the hills, she smiled a little sadly. She didn't have to wonder, she knew exactly how he would react. With a total lack of belief. So would Melly, so would anyone she tried to convince. Only Trent Addison, the man who had rescued her, knew why she had gone with him. That was why she was going to keep her silence, at least until she had worked out some plan.

'Where do you want to go?' Rafe's deep voice intruded into her thoughts.

Startled, she looked up and met his eyes in the rear vision mirror. When Melly spoke her voice seemed to shatter some potent, frightening spell.

'I just want to prowl around the boutiques,' she told him.

'Jennet?'

'I'll have a look in the craft shops,' she said a little huskily. 'What are you doing?'

'Seeing various people,' he said. 'I'll meet you at the Waterfront Café at one o'clock.'

It was not exactly an order, but Jennet had no intention of being even a minute late.

When the big Audi had been locked Melly walked swiftly across the parking lot, leaving Jennet to Rafe's mercies. He took her elbow to support her over the cracked, uneven asphalt; he must have felt her instinctive withdrawal for his fingers tightened.

'Are you buying gifts?' he asked unexpectedly.

The sun gleamed in soft fire on her hair. He was striding beside her with that flowing vitality which was so essential a part of him yet they were miles apart, distanced by the years and his dislike.

'No,' she said. 'I want to look at the pottery. It's a hobby of mine.'

'Is it?' He sounded surprised. His fingers slid down her arm to enclose her hand and he lifted it for inspection. 'Buying it, I presume. This delicate hand doesn't look as if it's ever done any work. Certainly not dabbling in clay on a potter's wheel.'

'You presume wrong,' she said, after clearing her throat. His touch was not in the least impersonal. Quite deliberately he was stroking her palm with his thumb and the gentle little caress made her feel as though her nerves were hot wires in her body.

With a cutting edge to her voice Jennet continued, 'I'm actually quite good. I learned to pot at school. In fact, I'm almost certain I gave you an ashtray one Cnristmas before you gave up smoking.'

'Yes, I think you did.' He sounded amused now, and arrogant and dismissive all at once. 'I was rather touched. Which is more than Diana was when you gave her a vase.'

The pain of her mother's light, almost scoffing dismissal of the little green vase had long faded, but her voice was uneven as she asked, 'Don't you ever forget anything?'

'Very little. Especially not a grudge. Or a woman I want.' His fingers tightened as she tried to pull free. 'And I have a lot of patience.'

Her lashes flicked nervously at the barely hidden warning. She had to force herself to look away from him and when she did, she could still see the cynical amusement which lay at the back of his eyes.

'You won't need patience,' she retorted, her voice thick.

'Good. Does that mean I can expect you in my bed tonight?'

Colour scorched up her throat and across her cheekbones. 'Can't you drag your mind any higher?' she asked crudely, and then flushed again.

Pleased, he grinned and said 'I'll see you at one,' and left her, walking down the street with long panther strides, the automatic focus of almost every passer-by.

Jennet turned her back, but his image was engraved on the retina of her eyes. He would photograph well. That magnificent bone structure would entrance the camera, and he had presence as well as looks which would come across too. Wondering viciously whether that unclassifiable air of sexual competence could be caught in film, she made her way to the craft shop.

Still deep in discussion with the proprietor, a lean, middle-aged woman with shrewd eyes and a tentative smile, Jennet jumped when Melly's voice broke in.

'Come on, Jen, it's time to go. Hello, Mrs Clarke.'

It was ten past one.

'Oh dear,' Jennet muttered after she'd fled from the shop. 'Oh Lord, is he frothing at the mouth?'

'I don't know. I'm late, too. He'll be very thin around the lips though. Are you still potting?'

'Yes.' Jennet blinked at the glare. At this time of the year the sun was at its lowest so the rays searched in under the verandah roofs.

'What sort of things do you make?'

'Oh, ewers and bowls, plates, that sort of thing.' Jennet was deliberately vague. She had no intention of revealing that her work sold quickly and for high prices, or that it was becoming sought after by an ever-increasing circle of connoisseurs.

The café was an old building but it had been renovated and cleverly redecorated in late Victorian style. Fronting on to the pavement it was built on piles out over the sea, in past years a not uncommon method of conserving the little available flat land. Rafe was talking to another man; when he saw them he nodded and came across to where they stood.

'We'll go out on to the balcony,' he said, and took Jennet's elbow again, not relinquishing it until they reached their table.

Beneath the wide boards of the balcony the sea washed softly in the wake of a small fishing boat which was making its way to the jetty. Seagulls flew in lazy circles above it, and on a pile of black shag one crouched, one wing spread out. Even in the brilliance of the sun it looked faintly sinister.

'What would you like to drink?'

Rafe gave their order to the young waitress, smiling at her with such virile charm that she blushed and had to ask for the order again.

They were attracting attention, Jennet realised with dry amusement as two teenaged girls passed by their table, their eyes swivelling in sidelong contemplation of Rafe. She didn't have to look far to find several appreciative masculine glances slanting from her to Melly.

Well, they made an eyecatching trio, the two Hollingworths so dark, she such a contrast. Two attractive women and a man who looked rather like every woman's secretly cherished dream of romance incarnate.

Of course Rafe wasn't in the least romantic. He was tough and arrogant with a temper bad enough to frighten away any sensible person, a brain as sharp as broken glass and a personality to match.

A small smile pulled at her mouth as she watched him deal smoothly with the by now flustered waitress. She'd better clean up her act, Jennet thought wryly; Rafe didn't suffer fools gladly. The blandly gracious demeanour could give way to a polite, cold ruthlessness in no time at all. Or was it only to his stepsister—and her mother—that he revealed that aggression? Perhaps no one else experienced anything beyond the cool sophistication which was the usual aspect of his many-faceted character.

The idea gave her an obscure pleasure she refused to dissect. Instead, she sipped Perrier water while she studied the menu.

'The seafood is good here,' he said.

Nodding, Jennet said, 'Well, that's what I'll have.'

'Scallops?'

She nodded again.

'And hapuka?' At her surprised look, he smiled narrowly. 'I told you I forgot nothing.'

'With a brain like that you don't need the computer I saw queening it over your office,' she retorted.

He grinned at that, tacitly calling a truce. 'I like computers. Besides, it stores an immense amount of information which I then don't have to worry about. Once it's in there it's in for good, and I can retrieve it instantly.'

'Good for you,' she said lightly. 'It must make the bookwork much easier. Is Wendy Hardy still your secretary?'

'Yes, although I'll have to look for someone else soon; unfortunately for me she is going to Hamilton to live with her daughter.'

The waitress came back with their first course, very earnest as she placed the dishes carefully in front of them.

For some reason Jennet remembered the flinty note which appeared in her mother's voice whenever she spoke of Te Puriri. Diana had hated living there, so far from Auckland. Eventually her constant complaints had driven Dougal to another life, and a job he hated in the city. No wonder Rafe despised what he saw as his father's weakness.

He was different; no woman would ever sway his

actions. Presumably he would marry one day to provide
Te Puriri with an heir, but even if he loved his wife she
would have to fit in with his life. There would be no
compromise; it was unlikely that Rafe admitted the
word to his vocabulary! His naturally dominating
personality had been hardened by the effects of the
flaws in Dougal's character.

As she ate the fat, sweet scallops in a white wine
sauce, Jennet dragged her attention back to the
conversation.

'. . . I'm sorry, I know you don't like them,' Melly
was saying, 'but I did promise Brigit we'd call in.'

'Then we'll go,' Rafe said. 'Don't look so distressed,
I'm not going to chew your ears off. I hope I can
remain polite to her for an hour or so.'

'Even when you're rude you're polite! She's not so
bad, you know. And it was you who said that we'd
better accept her invitation to dinner before the ball.
That was before Cathy said she couldn't come, of
course.'

He grinned, not in the least annoyed by the
imputation, before saying smoothly, 'Jennet can take
her place.'

'I beg your pardon?'

Something in his expression made her uneasy. 'You
can be my partner at the Mialls' party,' he told her,
those heavy-lidded eyes very sharp as they surveyed her
face. 'And the Settler's Ball afterwards. You'll be
staying for a couple more days, I presume.'

'Yes. Yes, of course. I haven't a ball dress, however.'

'Wear what you had on last night,' Rafe said. 'It
looked stunning.'

Melly said, 'As balls go it's not madly formal. We're
having dinner at the Mialls' first.'

'Sounds fun. Who are the Mialls?'

'Oh, a couple who live where Brownsons used to.'
Melly exchanged a complicated look with Rafe. 'He's a

property developer and they bought the station when John Brownson sold out.'

'Nice?'

'I'll let you make up your own mind.'

They were pleasant enough, if a little too conscious of their wealth and the Hollingworth's social position. Brigit Miall was a thin, small woman with the sharp eyes of the born gossip. She told an entertaining anecdote, as though she had decided to compensate for the deficiencies of her person by being the best-informed woman in her circle.

The Brownson's old homestead had been demolished and an enormous, extremely well-designed house set in its place. The old-fashioned gardens had been revamped into trendiness, with an enormous swimming pool and entertainment area so well sheltered that it was warm enough for them to be able to sit out and sip long, cool drinks.

And there, under the cynically amused gaze of Rafe, Brigit launched into the inevitable, delicately pursued inquisition. Jennet smiled and parried and answered, giving very little away.

Plainly Brigit knew of her. Equally plainly she wasn't sure of her position in the family.

Those inquisitive eyes darted from the chiselled aloofness of Rafe's handsome face to Melly's grave one and then back to Jennet, assessing, impertinent, even, Jennet decided warily, a trifle malicious. So she countered with a smooth charm acquired rather painfully in many encounters with reporters. When she cared to, Jennet could assume a certain stylish arrogance which was intimidating enough to keep the Brigit Mialls of the world in line.

After a while the older woman backed off and began to drop titbits of gossip into the conversation. There was an amusing dissection of someone's tangled love life followed by a brief, pungent and extremely intelligent rundown on another's financial affairs.

John Miall drew Rafe away to ask him something about the station and Melly sauntered across the terrace to where a small Burmese kitten played with a dead leaf.

'Nice to see Melly so—relaxed,' Brigit purred.

'Yes.'

'Yes, after last year's episode she seemed very triste. I began to wonder if she was ever going to get over it.'

Jennet's brows lifted as her eyes followed Melly's progress. 'Oh?' she said, on just the faintest note of encouragement.

'I suppose it wouldn't have worked out.' Brigit paused artistically. 'Trent is absolutely gorgeous, but he does have a bad reputation where women are concerned. He's one of our dearest friends, but I'm afraid Melly was out of her depth.'

For a moment the sunny garden wavered rather horribly in front of Jennet's eyes.

'Trent?' she managed in a level voice. 'That's an unusual name.'

'Isn't it. Very suited to its owner.' Brigit sounded slightly disappointed but she went on confidingly, 'Trent Addison is Derek's cousin. Didn't you ever meet him?'

Very coolly Jennet answered, 'Yes. Once or twice.' Ran away with him, too, but Brigit might not know of that.

She was acutely conscious of the razor sharp impact of the older woman's glance as she said, 'That's right, he and Derek don't get on too well, do they? It's a pity when families fight. I know when he was staying with us last year, he wouldn't go to see Derek. That's when he met Melly.'

Jennet said nothing. After a long moment Brigit continued, 'He became rather enamoured of her. And she of him, I thought. They saw quite a lot of each other for a couple of months and then pouff! it was over. Melly went to spend the holidays with her mother and Trent flung himself into his work.' She gave a little tinkling laugh. 'I've always suspected that Rafe had a hand in it. He wasn't very happy about the affair. Not that I believe that it was an affair, of course. Amusing, isn't it? Rafe just has to be a rake, yet he hasn't much time for others.'

'Not when his sister is concerned,' Jennet agreed lightly. 'But perhaps it just died a natural death.'

'Perhaps. Although I thought they were seriously smitten and I'm rather good at that sort of thing. Not that I asked, of course. Trent is a dear friend but not even I would have the gall to ask him about his love life. He and Rafe make a pair, don't they, magnificently macho and both are very definitely off-putting if anyone intrudes on their personal space.'

Jennet smiled, her serenely composed expression hiding the furious working of her brain. This, she thought exultantly, might be the information she needed to bulldoze a way through the tangle.

Of course Rafe had had something to do with the break-up of Melly's embryo love affair. He'd probably told her that Trent Addison was the man who had seduced Jennet away from Derek. And in a way he was right, although there had been nothing of an emotional nature between them. Trent had never even seen her as a desirable woman, only as one who needed help. A tall, lean devil with ice-grey eyes and hair the colour of mahogany, he was a rangy, piratical type who had been unexpectedly, devastatingly kind to her when kindness was the last thing she had expected. Not exactly good looking, she recalled, but the reputation Brigit gave him came as no surprise. Even in the emotionally dead state she had been in when he took her away from Derek, his intensely masculine appeal had registered.

Now she realised why Derek had chosen Melly for

his next wife, when he must have known that his engagement would bring Jennet back determined to do her best to prevent it.

Aloud, she murmured, 'Yes, I suppose there are points of resemblance between them.'

'Clever, too, both of them. Trent is a genius with electronics and computers and things like that. He's building himself an empire now, exporting.' Brigit paused. 'He's been overseas for the past six weeks, just got back three days ago. I had thought of inviting him to the ball . . .'

'Had you?' Jennet gave her the full benefit of widened eyes and a small, provocative smile. 'How nice. I like Trent.'

Yes, she had been correct in her summing up. The older woman was a mischief-maker. She smiled back, those sharp eyes bright with significance.

'Well, I'll see,' Brigit said.

But Jennet caught the swift anticipatory relish in the other's voice and knew that if Brigit Miall could swing it, Trent Addison would be there.

After that they chatted until Melly came back, inconsequential stuff that merely passed the time away. Perhaps it would be too harsh to say that Brigit gloated, but as Jennet watched the thin face, she realised that the older woman was eagerly looking to an evening which would provide her with enlivening gossip for some time to come. Of course, she would be banking on every one's good manners to prevent any dangerous emotions from getting out of hand. Brigit could well be too confident; she had obviously never encountered Rafe in a black mood.

But they would all behave in public with propriety, even Derek. They had had years to learn how to hide their feelings. Not that Rafe would hesitate to make a scene, but he had better methods of making his anger felt. Derek was definitely not the man to make a fuss in public. Other people's opinion, and his social standing, mattered very much to Derek.

But if, somehow, his equilibrium could be tilted, then perhaps . . .

A chill feathered across her skin. It would be dangerous, but it might be the only way to bring the situation to a head. If Trent really had meant something to Melly . . . if Derek hated his cousin enough . . . if Jennet could manipulate events and people . . .

Unconsciously she made a grimace of distaste. How hateful, to be plotting and planning like this. As the men came back she looked up to find Brigit watching her.

Not a comfortable woman, she thought, suddenly cold. Almost certainly, Brigit was feared as well as liked. And for all the clever flattery, the amusing, skilful dropping of names, she could not hide the envy which motivated her.

On the way home Rafe and Melly were silent. Once, looking up, Jennet caught Rafe's eyes in the rear-vision mirror. They gleamed like onyx, opaque, all thoughts hidden. She felt grubby and guilty, and glanced away quickly before he could pick up the emotions in her.

Te Puriri dreamed quietly in its hidden valley, surrounded by the steep green hills which gave it riches and security and a stake in the future. It looked like a land under an enchantment, locked in a stasis where nothing changed, nothing died.

Old emotions, the ghosts of the past; pain and anger and bitter hurt, betrayals and an obsessive love, hung heavily on the warm air as well as golden moments of joy and ecstasy and laughter.

I love it so, Jennet thought wearily. All my life it's all that I've ever wanted, and I'll never be anything more than an intruder.

Once back, she went out through the french windows of her bedroom on to the loggia where great cymbidium orchids in pots wove an exotic, peaceful spell. It was so hot that she collapsed on to one of the loungers and closed her eyes, wondering why she didn't leave, go straight back to Australia and spend the rest of this holiday with friends on the Gold Coast. Of course she couldn't, but oh, it seemed like the thought of Paradise to a dying woman.

A sudden memory from last night impelled her from the peace of the loggia to Melly's room. It was empty so Jennet drifted downstairs, finally catching up with her in the boudoir where she was curled up in a chair, reading.

'Where are you and Derek planning to live when you're married?' Jennet asked after a small amount of preliminary conversation.

Melly looked both suspicious and taken aback.

'Derek's bought a farm south of Te Kuiti,' she amswered slowly. 'In the depths of the King Country.'

A quick mental survey of the map brought a frown to Jennet's brows. 'But that's at the back of beyond,' she objected.

'Don't you see me as a pioneer?'

Jennet sat down, smiling. 'Tell me all about it,' she invited.

At any other time she would have been amused at the combination of eagerness and caution which struggled for supremacy in Melly's expression. Finally, however, the desire to confide won.

'Well, it's miles from civilisation,' she said. 'It's right at the end of a back road towards the coast, and it's only partly brought in. Derek says it's beautiful, pretty steep in places with lots of bush on it but it's going to take us a long time to bring it all in. Derek is really looking forward to the challenge. He finds Compton Downs too tame,' she finished defiantly. 'And so do I.'

'Do you know anyone there?'

'Well, no, but people are bound to be friendly. They

usually are in an isolated community like that.' She paused, her dark eyes, so like her brother's searching Jennet's face. As if dissatisfied with whatever she saw there, she continued, 'The house is old, but sound. Derek says we'll live in it for a year to see what we want, and then have the basics done, plumbing, a new kitchen, and then, he says, we'll probably have to make do for some years as all the money will be going back into the place.'

Again there was that note of defiance in her voice. To Jennet it sounded as though, learning from the mistakes he had made in his first marriage, Derek was all set to make sure that this wife couldn't leave him.

Appalled, but unable to show it, she asked casually, 'How many men will he need to work for you?'

'Well, for a few years, none. It will be more economic to bring in contractors and we won't be able to afford to build housing for any workers straight off. Eventually, of course, we'll need at least two, Derek thinks.'

Jennet felt sick. Vaguely she said, 'Well, good luck to you,' as she got to her feet with far less than her usual grace.

'Jennet.'

Something in Melly's voice made her stiffen. Without looking at her half-sister she answered, 'Yes?'

'You won't be welcome there, you know. You've done enough damage. Just leave him alone.' The cool voice trembled. 'If you could have seen what he was like after you left him, well, even you would have felt guilty, I'm sure. He's happy now and so am I. There's nothing you can do to break us up so why don't you give up trying?'

A quick glance was revealing. Melly had had to steel herself to say this much, but her gaze was perfectly steady and she meant every word of it, the young face set in lines which recalled her brother at his most determined.

Jennet admired her and wished achingly that she had come back on any other mission than this. But she hardened her heart and her voice, saying mockingly, 'Nothing can come between true lovers, didn't you know that, Melly? So why are you worried?'

'I'm *not* worried!'

Jennet laughed and continued out of the room, only stopping to give her sister's rigid unresponsive shoulders a hug. 'I do love you,' she said, and she meant it.

All the years when she had resented the small sister who had taken her place in her mother's heart, were dissipated like spindrift. A bitter sense of responsibility had driven her back to Te Puriri and she had come resentfully, but now she was imbued with a rediscovered affection for her half-sister.

'Remember when I pushed you into the pool so that I could practise my life-saving on you?' she asked from the door. 'You gave me a black eye for my pains, but when I cried from sheer frustration you drowned very sweetly about ten times to make up for it.'

Melly stared at her as if she had gone mad before saying stiffly, 'Yes, I remember. I'm surprised you do, though.'

'Oh, I remember lots. You'd be astounded!'

'Nothing would surprise me about you.'

Rafe's deep voice made her jump and for a moment real fear showed in her face. Within seconds she had banished it, but Melly stared, her astonishment written large in her expression.

'Oh, compliments, compliments,' Jennet mocked in her warmest, throatiest voice as she flashed a smile at the man behind her. 'Darling, you're looking rather grim. Lost a sheep or something?'

The straight sensual mouth relaxed into a smile which came perilously close to a snarl.

'No, darling,' he said, his voice very even. 'Nothing so simple, I'm afraid.'

'Ah well, I'm going to sunbathe. Do you still heat the pool?'

'We do.'

She smiled slowly and with infinite promise into his face, meeting the cold anger of his eyes with teasing amusement. 'Then I'll go and swim,' she said lightly.

CHAPTER FIVE

THE pool was another piece of Italiannate design, an elegant pretty place copied, so rumour had it, from something the builder of the house had seen in the ruins of Pompeii. It was white and there were pillars and statues of rather winsome goddesses and impertinent fauns, even a fountain which glistened and glinted in rainbow colours in the sun. The water was warm, but not enervatingly so. Jennet swam purposefully from end to end, her graceful body belying the strength and stamina she possessed. After she climbed out, she showered in the changing room and pulled out a lounger into the sun, being careful to anoint herself with a total sunblock before she lay down.

Not for her the ease with which Melly and Rafe tanned. Her skin was the sort which is prone to skin cancer; she would have liked to spend much more time in the sun but common sense warned her of the dangers. Here, as in Australia, she sunbathed with care.

However, before she had time to relax completely in the drowsy warmth she felt a shadow fall over her face. Slowly, reluctantly, she opened her eyes.

Rafe, of course, that onyx gaze leisurely assessing her body, lingering with insufferable enjoyment on the rounded curves of breasts and waist, the slender length of her legs, the seductive body hidden only by the thin white material of her maillot.

'You look,' he said cruelly, 'like an advertisement for virginity. Even to the blush!'

'Well, you'd probably be surprised by the number of men who are turned on by it,' she retorted flippantly, hating, yet strangely excited by, his open, lustful scrutiny.

'I doubt it. I find you eminently desirable myself,' he drawled, letting his glance linger on the areas of her body which revealed only too clearly how and why she appealed to him. In the most basic of ways, merely to appease an animal lust.

The colour across Jennet's cheeks deepened into a scalding flood. She felt like slapping his face, but even as her hands straightened she regained control. Whatever happened, she was not going to blow everything by losing her temper.

He knew, too. She could · read the taunting amusement in his eyes as he turned away to haul his shirt over his head.

Stripped, he was—well, superb was the only word. Skin the texture of bronze silk stretched over muscles which flexed as he moved lithely, with arrogant grace. Jennet watched him from beneath her lashes, her mouth drying. Like those statues of Greek warriors, she thought feverishly, a magnificent amalgam of strength and grace and balance. Her lashes drooped. She wiped suddenly damp palms with surreptitious care on the cushions of the lounger and turned over on to her stomach, pressing her face into her arm.

There was no sound until a soft splash revealed that he was in the pool. Grimly Jennet kept her eyes closed, fighting the sensations which wracked her body. It had been a long time since she had suffered them; the last time had been years ago when he had kissed her and caressed her and she, naïve little adolescent that she had been, had offered him the responses of her untaught innocence.

Ever since then, because his rejection had scarred, she had refused to admit that she could feel desire, had repressed the sensual side of her nature. It had been one of the reasons why her marriage failed.

And if she opened herself to him again that was exactly what would happen again. So she wanted him.

So what? It was ultimately degrading, but the body has its own law, its own immutable instincts. Which didn't mean that she had to give in to them.

Or perhaps she should. All these years she had backed away from the memories of her childish crush on him and the disillusionment that had followed his casual cruelty, his careless handling. By hiding from the implications she had, perhaps, allowed the incident to become too important. After all, he had been only twenty-three, sophisticated for his age, but still a young man. Had he been clumsy with her because he just didn't know how to handle the situation?

As the sounds of his progress up and down the pool kept her conscious of his presence she tried to recall exactly how he had behaved. And reluctantly she decided that he had known exactly what he was doing.

He had been punishing Diana because Dougal had loved her more than he had Rafe's dead mother. His rejection of Jennet had been one way of denying Diana's influence on his life, of working through his frustrated anger and resentment at the woman who had enslaved his father.

Rafe, so logical, so cool-headed, was a little bit unbalanced when it came to Diana, almost certainly because his attitude towards her had been formed in childhood, in the period of intense grief after his mother's death. Hating the woman who had taken her place with a fierce emotion based on instinct, he had included her daughter in that hatred because the daughter looked like the mother and had arrived with her.

Subsequent events had only reinforced his attitude, she thought sadly. It was impossible that they should ever know each other as ordinary people.

Her reverie was interrupted by the sounds of his leaving the pool.

As he dried himself down he asked shortly, 'Do you still want to see Derek?'

'Yes, I do.' She wanted to judge just how uneasy Derek was.

'He's here now.'

Yawning, she turned over on to her side, away from him. It was unlikely that Melly would give them time together; better, anyway, to assess him without the possibility of someone overhearing.

'It will wait,' she said lightly.

'I hope you're not expecting anyone to run you around when the fancy takes you. We work, you know.'

'I know you do.' An irritating note of laughter lilted in her tone. 'Don't worry about me, Rafe, I don't need to be entertained. I'm quite capable of amusing myself.'

There was an ominous pause and when he spoke again he was considerably closer. 'Not with Compton, I hope.'

'Oh, don't be so boring,' she shot back. 'You don't have to repeat things more than once, Rafe. I'm not thick.'

'No, just childish,' he said blightingly.

She tensed as he flung her over on to her back.

'A permanent adolescent,' he said. 'Like your mother, greedy, amoral, with a child's selfish outlook and a child's lack of foresight.'

She yawned again, pretending, half closing her eyes so that he couldn't see the pain in them.

'Think what you like,' her voice was indifferent. 'Your opinion means nothing to me.'

'Do you think I don't know that?' He leaned over her, harshly chiselled features drawn into bleak lines which didn't ease when he saw the alarm flare into her eyes. 'You hate me—and fear me—because I'm one of the few men who can see right through that intoxicating femininity you use as a cloak to hide the mean little soul inside.'

He meant every word yet there was something else behind the controlled distaste, something just as potent.

'Yes,' he said with a savage inflection as he sat down beside her on the lounger. 'There's that, too.'

'I don't——'

'You lie. It's lust, and you feel it just as I do.'

Before she could react his mouth came to rest on the swell of her breast, burning through the thin dampness of her maillot. Jennet struck out at him but his fingers fastened cruelly around her elbows, forcing her arms on to the mattress and holding her still.

'No!' she ground out while her body melted into acquiescence. 'You're a swine, Rafe, a bully. Let me go.'

He lifted his head and grinned, a feral mirthless movement of his hard mouth. 'I like having you at my mercy.'

'Brute!'

He kept her pinned with the crystalline intensity of his glare, his eyes roving her face in an insulting scrutiny. 'You know, you're not really beautiful. Your features are neither classical nor cute, your eyes are too big and your mouth too wide and yet you simmer with a sexuality which stops even happily married men in their tracks. Poor old John Miall had to get out before Brigit noticed.'

'Brigit notices everything!'

'So do I,' he said smoothly as his mouth covered hers, coaxing it to open.

Just in time Jennet clenched her teeth, saying bitterly, 'You can't do this to me. I'm not one of your women, to be toyed with and then discarded like a worn-out doll.'

'No, you're a permanent part of my life. Almost part of me.'

So astounded was she by this, delivered in his most reasonable tones, that she gaped. Half a second later she appreciated his strategy as his mouth invaded hers in a kiss totally without subtlety or tenderness. He wanted her and he didn't care if he hurt her; his desperate kiss fed a brutal sensuality which should have repelled Jennet. For a few stark seconds it did. She went rigid beneath him, her whole being suffused with outrage.

Then, as if his ferocity had breached some hidden barrier, a great wave of heat surged through her body. She sighed and his arms slid beneath her suddenly pliant body, lifting her so that she lay against him. Her lashes fluttered down as she was stricken by a kind of sensory overload. The warm male scent of him, the rapid heating of his skin against hers made her groan. Circles of sparks danced behind her eyelids and her mouth was filled with the taste of him, erotic, stimulating.

A convulsive tremor shook her. Slowly she brought her hands up to clasp his shoulders.

He delighted her, he was perfect to her.

'I could get drunk on the look of you,' he whispered harshly, 'on the taste of you, the perfume of your skin and hair. I could drown in your eyes.'

His voice was thick with longing and need. Across her back his arms tightened so that she felt as if it had happened to her, the tremor which shook him. Slowly she opened her eyes to focus on his face, drawn in a mask of anguish.

'Why?' she breathed, afraid yet exultant. 'Why, Rafe?'

'God knows.' It sounded like a curse. 'It's the same for you, isn't it?'

It was too painful to watch him, stripped of self-possession, naked in his hunger for her.

'Oh yes,' she said, closing her eyes as she nodded, weak with supplication and the urgency of the need he had aroused.

'Why did you come back?' he asked against her throat.

She froze, every process in her body suspended.

Oh, he was clever, bending even his passion to serve his will. As her eyes stared blindly over his dark hair she realised with bleak comprehension that he had baited a trap for her, using the heated sexuality of their desire for each other to strip her bare of lies and evasions.

Then from behind came Melly's voice, shocked and furious, its strident edge cutting through the warm sleepy air. 'My God!' she exclaimed, as though she had discovered a sin hitherto uncatalogued. 'What are you doing?'

For a precious, secret moment Rafe's black gaze met Jennet's and in both pairs of eyes was mirrored a kind of guilty amusement.

Then Rafe straightened up and put Jennet back on to the cushions of the lounger as he said in a voice totally devoid of expression, 'What does it look as though we're doing?'

'Oh, Rafe!' Melly said sadly before she turned and left them.

Rafe laughed, a cynical, humourless sound and raked his hand through his hair, staring down at Jennet as though he hated her. Then, without a further word, he swung on his heel and left.

No doubt telling himself that he was a fool, she thought drily. As she was. Stupid to respond to his lovemaking, stupid to let him get to her. Stupid, stupid, *stupid*!

A short while later she came quietly down the stairs, her jean-clad legs suddenly tired. She had planned to prowl around the gardens but swimming and the passionate scene afterwards had exhausted her. Now, she listened carefully for voices, deducing after a moment that Derek and Melly were in the sitting-room. Silently she walked past it to the library.

Nothing had changed here except for the replacement of a pair of Japanese vases by a magnificent pottery bowl in subtle shades of green and grey. She was still admiring it, her hands smoothing tenderly over the thin transparent glaze when the door opened behind her.

Derek, his handsome face set in an expression perilously close to smugness.

'Aha, caught you!' he said with a smile which did not extend to his eyes. 'If you're planning to abscond with some loot, I'd choose something else. Take that porcelain jardiniere. It's Chinese, so Melly says, and worth a couple of thousand dollars.'

Replacing the bowl on its stand Jennet said calmly, 'In two hundred years time this will be worth as much.'

Derek's jaw tightened. With a heady sense of power which was unpleasantly exciting, Jennet realised that he was a little afraid of her.

'What can I do for you?' she asked politely.

He grinned, coming to stand too close in front of her, his bright eyes scanning her face.

'You know why I'm here,' he said insolently and lifted his hand and traced the soft curve of her mouth.

'Do I?' Her voice was steady. She was trying to cope with a strange feeling of *déjà vu*, as though this had happened before, many times. A thin, savage anger sparkled in the green depths of her eyes as her expression hardened into lines which made her look much older, much stronger.

Derek's hand dropped and he stepped back. 'Oh, I think you do,' he said easily. 'You're having a little financial trouble, I gather.'

'Actually, no.' She enjoyed his surprise, quickly hidden though it was. 'Soap operas may not be the height of culture, but they pay well. You can't buy me off, Derek. You couldn't before, if you remember, and I'm a lot better off now than I was then.'

'I see.'

As he paused, trying to work out his next move, she said blandly. 'Why don't you sit down and tell me all about your new property?'

'Who told—oh, Melly, I suppose.'

'Yes.' She sat down gracefully on to one of the big armchairs, waited with polite enquiry while he subsided, with less than his normal grace, into one opposite her. 'You know, anyone who was the least suspicious would think that you intend carrying Melly off to the backblocks so that she can't run away from you.'

'Why should she want to?'

She smiled but there was no amusement in her eyes. 'The same reason that I ran away?' she suggested.

He frowned. 'I love Melly,' he said quickly.

Jennet eyed him from beneath her lashes. Somewhat to her surprise she was inclined to believe him and for a moment she wondered hopefully if she could trust him enough to be free of this burden she had imposed on herself.

Just for a moment until the psychiatrist's dry, dispassionate words came back to her.

'I wonder,' she said calmly, 'what Rafe would do to the man who harmed Melly—in any way?' She watched him swallow before continuing mercilessly, 'Do you think Rafe would murder, Derek?'

He said quickly, 'No, he's a civilised man and anyway why should I harm Melly? I love her, I tell you. She's everything you're not, warm, passionate, loving.' He smiled at her start of surprise and added triumphantly, 'That surprises you, doesn't it. You're so bloody frigid yourself you can't understand how Melly could get carried away——'

'I've always heard that it's frightfully bad form to kiss and tell,' she said with cool deliberation. 'Rafe wouldn't.'

He flushed, the blood running up under his fair skin in a wave of colour and said through gritted teeth, 'You're asking for——'

'And anyway,' she interrupted, 'I don't believe you.'

'Why not?'

He reacted with the same touchy antagonism that had always been his response when found out in a lie. Jennet's relief was profound, but well disguised.

'Because you don't look at each other as lovers do,' she said calmly. 'You're still hungry and Melly is still unaware.'

'Oh, so you can tell just by looking?'

She sent him a level, dispassionate look. 'I know Melly and I understand you.'

For some reason this made him flush again. She didn't speak and he sat, uncomfortable and angry, a frown marring the handsome, weak face.

'So,' he said at last, 'where do we go from here? It's no use you filling Mel's ears with lies, you know. She won't believe anything you say. She's stubborn and she's in love with me.' He met her flat, unresponsive gaze with an anger which was stronger because he dared not vent it. 'Look,' he said, trying very hard to stay in control, 'you and I—well, we married for all the wrong reasons. That's so, isn't it?'

The rose-blonde head nodded slowly.

'Then can't you believe that—that I'm in love with Melly? I love her.'

Once more she nodded and he went on more easily now, 'Well, if that's so, why—what do you intend to do? Remembering that nothing you can do or say is going to make any difference.'

'What will you do the first time she makes you angry?' Jennet asked wearily.

He whitened. 'I'm five years older,' he said with such earnestness that she was tempted to believe him. Until she remembered again what the psychiatrist had said.

'I know,' she said. 'Believe me, I know, Derek. And I believe that you do love Melly, but I'm afraid I can't accept that you won't beat her when something happens to make you lose control. Just as you beat me. Have you ever been to a doctor about your propensity for violence?'

'No!' he shouted, suddenly furiously angry. 'Why should I? It was you, with your coldness, your frigid high-mindedness, your——'

He stopped, for Jennet was watching his hands as they curled and crooked, flexed into fists and then relaxed. When the impassioned words died away she lifted her eyes and regarded his distorted face with sorrow and regret. No fear, not a vestige of the sickening acrid terror which used to taste in her mouth whenever they quarrelled. Towards the end of their short marriage it had sprung to life whenever she had seen him.

Then he swore, savage, bitter obscenities which took him from the chair, to the window where he stood with his back to her, ramrod straight, his big hands clenched at his side while he fought for control.

He was, Jennet realised, afraid of her. Once he would have hit her but now he didn't dare and there was no way other than cursing that he could ease himself of the demons which drove him.

'Derek,' she said when the harsh monotone of his voice had died away, 'why don't you go to a doctor? They can help——'

'Because I don't need to!' He almost screamed the words. 'Because I'm not mad, damn you! Everything you got you deserved. You were in love with bloody Rafe when you married me and you're still in love with him! Do you think that did anything for my ego?'

'If you knew that—which was more than I did—why did you marry me?'

He jerked his head back as though she had hit him but still refused to look at her. 'I didn't know, then,' he said sullenly after a long hesitation.

She sighed, realising that she was unable to reach

him. But she had to try. 'If you went to see a doctor,' she began tentatively.

He was across the room and dragging her up from the chair before she had time to defend herself.

'No,' he said from between his teeth, his eyes lit by the manic glare she remembered. 'No, curse you, you conniving, double-crossing, lying bitch, I won't——'

He began to shake her, his fingers tightening like talons on the slender bones of her shoulders.

'I won't——' he swore just as the door opened and Rafe's deep cold voice demanded, 'What the *hell's* going on here?'

Derek flung her away from him, the frantic savagery wiped from his face as if it had never existed. Again Jennet was visited by that overpowering sense of *déjà vu*. This had happened the night Derek's cousin had come to visit them, the night before she had run away. In a second Derek had changed from an uncontrolled sadist to a reasonable, if angry man.

Now he turned and said loudly, 'If you don't want me to give your stepsister what she deserves, Rafe, exercise some control over her, will you? And tell her that I will not permit her or anyone else to come between Melly and me, not an ex-wife with an axe to grind, not even you.'

Oh, but he was clever! Even as he spoke Jennet's despairing eyes saw the suspicion fade in Rafe's hard face to be replaced by the intolerant contempt. Her chance of explaining just why she had come back to Te Puriri evaporated into the charged atmosphere. Rafe would never believe her now; it would have been hard enough to convince him at any time, but Derek's consummate skill at acting had cut the ground neatly away from under her feet. She didn't need his triumphant glance to see that he had chosen exactly the right approach to convince Rafe that she was interfering for the sheer delight of making mischief.

'Melly's in the boudoir,' Rafe said now, his grim expression a frightening contrast to the crystalline glitter beneath his dark lashes.

With a final victorious smile, slightly muted in case Rafe should catch it, Derek left the room. All this time Rafe had been watching Jennet, his eyes never leaving her face.

'Now,' he invited blandly as the door closed behind Derek, 'tell me what all that was about.'

Her sore shoulders lifted in a small but defiant shrug. 'Why should I? You've already made up your mind.'

'I'd like to hear your version, nevertheless.'

Angrily, humiliated by his icy restraint, she retorted bitterly, 'So that you can call me a liar all over again? No thanks, Rafe, I know when I'm up against a closed mind.' She gave a short harsh laugh. 'You've spent almost all of my life telling me how untrustworthy I am, how the fact that you like to kiss me disgusts you and makes you hate yourself. It surprises me that you even let yourself be angry when I do some other typically vulgar thing. After all, you know me so well, I'd have thought that you—that you——'

She stopped, shocked and frightened by the sudden quaver in her voice. Derek's violence had drained her of strength and she wasn't thinking straight. Time to end it.

'Oh, what's the use,' she said, turning away so that he couldn't see her face. In a voice dulled by the effort to overcome her anguish she finished, 'I think I might just go back to Sydney after all. My coming here was another mistake in a life liberally dotted with them.'

'Are you wallowing in self-pity?' he asked, apparently incredulous. 'Do I add feeling sorry for yourself to my list of character defects?'

'Don't mock me,' she said grittily.

'Sorry. Of course you feel sorry for yourself. You've been doing that ever since you realised that Diana was

fonder of Melly than she was of you. Ah—ah . . .' as
she turned on him with eyes like green flames in a taut,
white face.

'No,' he drawled sardonically, 'you're like the rest of
your sex, you don't mind dishing it out but it's a
different story when it comes to taking it, isn't it? Now,
do you want to show me how well you can drive?'

Thrown completely off balance by the change of
subject she stared at him before shrugging. 'Oh, all
right,' she said listlessly.

It was a disaster. He wouldn't let her drive the big
Audi, but insisted she try Melly's smaller vehicle, which
was not automatic. It was some years since Jennet had
used a gear lever, but on any other occasion she would
have coped, for she was a good driver.

Today, however, she missed gear changes, concen-
trated too hard on the clutch pedal and almost hit a
fence, then thoroughly demoralised, drove as poorly as
a nervous schoolgirl being taught by her older brother.

And beside her, silent but ominous, Rafe said
nothing until she finally managed to stop the car inside
the garage.

Then he said 'No,' and refused curtly to listen to her
excuses or pleas, striding off into his office with a rude
lack of courtesy which ordinarily would have made her
furious.

This time, however, she merely watched his tall, lean
form pace up to the house and felt only an intense
weariness.

It lasted, aided by a headache, until she went to bed
an hour later, but when she woke the next morning it
had gone and she felt a little revived.

Breakfast with a silent, mistrustful Melly was not
pleasant. Afterwards Jennet made her bed and tidied
her room, once more offered help to Joy and once more
had it more or less refused, and decided to go for a
walk. Rafe had eaten early and was, so the housekeeper

informed her, out working somewhere on the station; Joy had packed him lunch which meant that he wasn't likely to be back much before dark.

It was a relief to leave the house. Melly's attitude created a tension which roughened Jennet's nerves. No doubt the incident at the pool was half the cause of Melly's antagonism, but Jennet rather suspected that Derek had stirred coals too. She couldn't unfortunately come right out and ask. Melly would have every right to tell her to mind her own business.

Pondering on the fact that Rafe had been surprisingly easily diverted after walking in on her with Derek the day before, Jennet wondered uneasily why he hadn't tried to pry from her the background to the scene he had interrupted. In any other man it might have been forbearance, but Rafe was not forbearing.

It was a superb day, one of those rare winter days which were warmer and more promising than most that spring could produce. The air was soft and mild, the sky blue, a tender, warm colour far removed from the crystalline hue that a south wind brought with it. What little breeze there was, came whispering in from the north-east, carrying on it a hint of the tropical isles of Polynesia.

Jennet stuck her hands in the pockets of her jeans as she sauntered along the drive. Te Puriri was a place apart, she thought dreamily, watching the antics of two courting tuis among the amber berries of an enormous melia tree. The big birds fluttered from silver branch to silver branch, glossy black wings and tails spread so that their burnished lustre of blue and green gleamed in the sunlight.

Jennet smiled as she opened the small gate beneath the tree and stood motionless, her eyes scanning the smiling fertile valley with its sheltering hills making bold statements against the sky. The drive ran down past the implement sheds and barns, all the necessary buildings of a big station, on past the houses each set in its own garden, and over a stream to pass the big woolshed at the gate. Beyond the gate was Compton Downs; by some quirk of surveying Derek's station bordered Te Puriri although the homestead was five miles away by road.

Compton Downs was in good heart, too, Jennet decided, eyeing what paddocks she could see with a critical gaze. Whatever financial troubles had prompted Derek's marriage to her had obviously been surmounted, but to buy a new block, however undeveloped, would be more than his resources allowed.

When she had lived with him she had not been allowed to know of his financial state. However she was not unintelligent and it had needed only his first outburst when he discovered that she almost literally had no money to her name, for her to realise that he needed money. Well, she thought angrily, if he married Melly he would get her income, but he had no power to break the trust as it was settled on her children. Dougal had made it watertight.

She knew then that she would have to try once more to convince Derek to see a doctor or psychiatrist. If he was adamant in his refusal then she would just have to work out some way of opening Melly's—or Rafe's—eyes to the tragic flaw in his character.

Why not now, she asked herself, her eyes narrowing as they came to rest on the station utility parked outside the implement shed. Away from Rafe's intimidating presence she could drive the wretched thing quite easily. If she missed a few gear changes, well, it was sturdily built and forgiving, and the roads in Takapo Valley were usually distinctly empty of traffic.

'Up guards and at 'em,' she said to the tuis, one of which answered with a distinct chirrup and a little song like a chime of bells.

A blackbird, resplendent in jet plumage with orange

beak and feet, took umbrage at the sound of her voice and flew shrieking away, frightening itself into a nervous breakdown.

'You, too,' she said aloud before she straightened her shoulders and strolled casually down the drive, looking around with real pleasure.

Rafe's love for his land was plain. It showed in the taut, trim fences, the new red paint on the shed and barns, the neat, well-cared for aspect of everything. There were unexpected touches too. A clump of red-hot-pokers had been fenced off so that stock couldn't eat the leaves. Against the lush green of the paddocks the pointed flowers glowed like coals of fire, each cone arrowing towards the sky. Another tui thrust its blue-black head deep into the long throat of one of the flowers then emerged to shake its head and display the white collar and bobble at its throat.

Jennet took a deep breath, forcing her mind away from the coming confrontation. A cluster of red and white Hereford cattle watched her solemnly, their heads turning as they followed her progress past them.

In the next paddock a small flock of newly shorn sheep, looking oddly long in the leg, ignored her. Any day now the first lambs were due; soon the paddocks would be full of the tiny, spring-heeled animals. A horse in a cover stood swishing its tail beneath a big old oak tree which was still tawny with old, unfallen leaves. The next blow would sweep them away and before long the tree would be radiant in its new clothes of vivid lime green.

As she came to the truck Jennet had to repress the desire to take a quick, furtive look around. Someone had obligingly parked it just where the drive began to slope quite steeply, so that she wouldn't even have to start it. She could free-wheel down the hill and when it had picked up enough speed a turn of the key and she'd be in business and at least a third of the way to the gate.

Well out of reach of anyone who might decide to see what she was up to.

Trying not to appear in the least stealthy, she climbed into the cab, closing the door with a quick sharp clunk which seemed to echo from every hill.

But no one appeared, no voice shouted, 'What do you think you're doing in that?'

'So far so good,' she told the unresponsive steering wheel.

Yes, the keys were in the ignition. Jennet took a deep breath, instantly regretting it. Although in excellent order the years had given the cab an interesting scent, a mixture of dog and fertiliser and other untraceable odours.

Nose wrinkled, Jennet eased off the handbrake. This time she held her breath as slowly, painfully slowly, the vehicle inched forward. When it began to pick up speed she grinned and patted the steering wheel.

Just in case someone lurked in the woolshed she didn't try to start it until she was over halfway down the hill, but when she did the engine struggled into life. Her grin broadened. As though she had spent her life stealing utilities she eased back into the seat.

The engine wheezed, sounding painfully asthmatic. Frowning, she listened for any further evidence of illness, but nothing eventuated. It was probably, she decided complacently just its usual noise. It certainly felt perfectly normal, although it was harder to drive than any car she had ever tried. The wheel had to be wrestled around as she took the corner at the bottom of the hill, and when she braked before heading over the bridge the vehicle jerked and almost skidded. Nervousness, she told herself, grinning.

And then there was a loud 'whoosh' and the engine exploded into a gush of flames and smoke.

Jennet panicked. She jerked the gear lever into the neutral position and slammed her foot hard down on to the brake. Fingers slippery with sweat fought with the wheel as she aimed the utility over the bridge, bringing it to a sliding, skidding halt on the other side.

Scrabbling for the door handle, she could hear the sound of her own whimpering. Smoke billowed back into the cab, choking her, making it impossible to see where the keys were. Half-remembered photographs of burn victims made her cry out in terror.

Then the door crashed back, hurtling her out. Rafe's hands provided further impetus so that she landed on her hands and knees some distance away, her eyes dilating in horror as she saw him disappear into the smoke.

'Rafe!' she screamed after a dreadful second.

He leaped back from the cab and she realised that he'd grabbed the fire extinguisher. There was an odd hissing noise, a cloud of strange-smelling stuff and then silence as foam enveloped the engine.

Shivering, Jennet crouched on the stones, her face hidden in her hands. She could not face Rafe's demonic fury, but there was no way she could shut out the sound of his voice as he told her exactly what he thought of her, only stopping when the manager came tearing up in the Land-Rover.

Reaction, Jennet told herself, wincing. Her body shook with long, slow rigours; she noticed with a vague interest that her skin was cold and clammy. Head bent she waited meekly until Rafe ran down.

Then as she got to her feet she asked shakily, 'But what happened? It was perfectly all right until——'

'It was *not* perfectly all right. How in hell did you start it?'

'I free-wheeled it down the hill until I got down by the totara tree.' She pointed. 'That one.'

He pushed shaking fingers through his hair, closing his eyes momentarily.

'Trust you,' he said bitterly. 'The fuel line was split,

that was what was wrong with it. I noticed it when it wouldn't start this morning.' His eyes fixed hers with such shimmering rage that she took an involuntary step backwards.

Slowly he looked above her head, saying in a voice which strove for calm, 'God damn it, I only left it to walk down to the woolshed. Some great idiot, whom I'll tear limb from limb, has taken the spanners from the implement shed. It's such a lovely day that I decided to walk to the shed to get the other set. I'd barely got there when I heard it start . . .'

From behind Jennet the farm manager told him apologetically, 'I think Evan's got the spanners.'

He went into details which Jennet didn't hear, because of the humming in her ears. After a moment or two she tried shaking her head. It made her feel better but it also switched Rafe's attention back to her.

'Why?' he demanded, biting the words out. 'Why did you want the truck?'

'Well you won't let me drive anything else,' she shouted, suddenly and completely losing command. 'You said——' To her horror her voice shook so much that she couldn't continue. Sudden rainbows filled her eyes as the sun glittered through her tears.

'Oh, *hell*!' Rafe's voice was totally disgusted. 'All right, Jennet, stop it. Rick, take us back to the house, will you?'

By now Jennet was sobbing in real earnest. Rafe stalked beside her until she stumbled, then, cursing under his breath, he slid an arm about her shoulders and held her clamped to his side until they got to the Land-Rover. Boosting her into the seat, he rapped out, 'You'd better drive,' to the farm manager as he got in beside her.

CHAPTER SIX

NOBODY spoke on the way back to the homestead. Indeed, the only sound inside the Land-Rover was the stifled sound of Jennet's weeping. Rafe no longer held her but she was close enough to him to feel the rage emanating from every taut contour of his body.

At the homestead he let her get herself out of the vehicle while he said something to the farm manager, but as Jennet began to trail miserably into the house he told her angrily, 'I want a few words with you.'

She shivered, knowing what was coming. He was going to tear strips from her and enjoy doing it. The years slipped away and she was sixteen again and he was going to deliberately shred her confidence, wounding her so deeply that she would never recover from it.

'The office,' he ordered sharply, still beside the Land-Rover.

As she made her way there Jennet tried to summon up some courage. All right, so she had been a—little impetuous—but no one could have expected the blasted utility to burst into flames. Could they? And yes, she had disobeyed him. But who was he to tell her what she might and might not do?

Within a short time her tears were gone and she was, to all outward appearances, composed. A composure which fled the minute he slammed into the office and straight into the attack.

'You stupid little *bitch*!' He was so angry that the words barely made it between lips as pale as the rest of his face. 'I should have let you kill yourself out there. What the *hell* made you take the bloody truck on the one day when it could have killed you!'

She was so shaken that the truth came out. 'I wanted to see Derek.'

Instantly that white rage deepened, intensified. His eyes were like slivers of obsidian, glittering, slicing her to ribbons.

'Can't you stay away from him for one day?' he demanded in the silky voice of extreme rage.

'I wanted to see him. Alone.' It took all of her precarious self-control not to shrink back into the sofa. She had never seen him like this before.

'You're sick,' he said terribly. 'Sick, promiscuous——'

'*No!*' She launched herself at him, fists flailing. 'No, no, *no*! I am not! How dare you—how *dare* you——'

His response was automatic and painful. Her voice sobbed into silence as his long fingers clamped around her wrists, but anger fuelled the kick she landed on his shin. He swore and dragged her against him, his arms tightening across her back.

Sobbing, her face smothered in his heavy shirt she choked, 'You—I'm not sick and I'm not promiscuous. I'm not, I'm not! I'm not Diana, I'm me. What have I ever done to you to make you hate me so?'

'Shut up,' he said disdainfully and when she gulped and gasped for breath the hand pressing her face into his shoulder relaxed and he let her go.

'You look like your mother,' he said icily, 'you project the same potent sensuality. I saw my father broken by a lust he couldn't control and I vowed that it was never going to happen to me.'

'But it almost did, didn't it,' she said painfully. 'Is that why you dislike me so, Rafe? Because I almost proved that you were just as vulnerable to lust as your father?'

Incredibly he laughed, a sound totally without humour before he put her away from him. She watched as he walked over to the fireplace and stared down into the faintly glowing coals.

'Of course,' he said politely. 'You came home from school those holidays and I watched you unfurl like an exquisite flower into a frightening, but completely familiar, beauty. Diana at sixteen. And I knew how my father must have felt when he first saw her. As if he'd been translated into another world where the normal code of ethics doesn't hold.'

'You never even saw me.' Her precarious confidence cracked, was shattered into a million pieces.

He leant an arm along the mantel, resting his forehead on to his wrist. 'Of course I saw you, how could I not? You swam, you sat at the table, you rode. And I had to listen to Diana keep up a constant stream of propositions, trying to seduce me while my father was hanging on to life by the thinnest of threads. She filled me with disgust but you——' He turned his head to look at her, his expression brooding, bitter. 'Oh, I could feel myself going under. I dreamed of you. I woke aching and famished for the sight and feel of you. I told myself I wanted to get you to bed, take you as roughly and quickly as possible, use you to slake a hunger I was ashamed of. But I lied to myself. I wanted more. I wanted to crack open your skull so that I could see what your beautiful, shuttered little face was hiding.'

Appalled by his cold, dispassionate recital of his emotions she said quietly, 'So you took your frustrations out on me.'

'No, although you'll never know how close you drove me to it.'

'*I* drove you?' Anger splintered in her voice. She came swiftly across to stand in front of him, her eyes blazing. 'I didn't start it, you did. I remember——'

Then she stopped for he was smiling, a savage feral movement of his mouth, while something glittered deep in his eyes.

'So do I,' he murmured. 'I remember it very clearly.'

She should have run then, turned and fled when she

had the freedom. But she stared at him, mesmerised, and he caught her close, his arm across her hips forcing her to the realisation that he was aroused.

'No,' she cried, terrified.

'Why not? You're not a scared virgin now and God knows, there's no reason for me to hold back. I still want you.'

Ignoring the hands which pushed at his shoulders he took her mouth, forcing her head back in a kiss as brutal and unforgiving as death's. Yet in spite of the insolence of it she responded, her body wracked by an unfamiliar chill.

'No,' she moaned when his head lifted a fraction and he smiled and kissed her again, searching out the secret depths of her mouth, his own ravenous.

Her heart thudded in her chest, picking up speed until the sound of it in her pulse points deafened her. His dark face filled her vision. She closed her eyes and instantly sensation was heightened, intensified to a degree beyond pleasure. She felt the heat of his body and the tense strength of it as he swayed her backwards so that she overbalanced and had to grab him, her fingers fiercely tangling in the material of his shirt.

Then when she thought she might faint with excitement and the strange, hot sensations raging through her he released her and the contempt darkened in his eyes as he looked at her.

'Just like Diana,' he said coolly. 'Beautiful and totally without discrimination.'

How she did it she never knew but even before she thought them the words issued from her lips delivered as a taunt.

'Oh, credit me with some discrimination,' she said lightly, prudently removing herself from arm's reach. 'I'm not propositioning you, you may have noticed. Call the kisses the hero's reward for saving me from a nasty death. Next time I'll tip you. It won't be so painful.'

He had recovered as quickly as she. With a smile which blended irony and contempt he retorted, 'Or so damaging to your make-up.'

So he had the last word after all. But as Jennet walked with bent head up the stairs to her bedroom she thought over the revelations Rafe had made. Her first reaction, now that she was alone, was shock. Just sheer shock.

For long minutes she sat on the side of her bed, her eyes fixed unseeingly on the hands in her lap as she remembered, caught once more in the past's snare. The egoism of childhood had blinded her to the knowledge, but of course Rafe had always been an intruder in his own home. On Diana's arrival the tall, proud boy who would one day own Te Puriri had been relegated to a lesser status and the pain of his father's rejection must have cut deeply.

After Melly's birth Diana had been unable to have more children. If she had borne Dougal a son even Te Puriri could have been denied Rafe. Where Diana was concerned Dougal had been weak, unable to deny her anything. At her insistence he had left his heritage for a life in Auckland which was unsatisfying. He had forced Rafe to buy the station which should have been rightfully his.

When Diana had denied convention to live with Dougal as his wife Rafe had been nine, old enough to fiercely resent any woman who took his mother's place. And Diana had never attempted to win his affection or his respect. Totally secure in the power her sensuality gave her over Dougal she had treated his son with the same callous forbearance she had given to Jennet. Her casual indifference was as shattering to a child as open unkindness, although there had been occasional instances of that, too. Diana was not particularly cruel; she just didn't care.

Stupidly, uselessly, Jennet's heart ached for the Rafe she only just remembered, the grave, silent boy who had, like her, been packed off to boarding school as early as possible. Born tough, those years had hardened his basic character even further.

It's no wonder, she thought drearily, that Melly is the only one of us he can stand. Possessive, made more so by the events of his childhood and Diana's machinations, he loved Melly because she was a Hollingworth; she belonged.

Incredulously, Jennet realised that she was crying. Not noisily, just sitting on her bed with the silent tears running down her cheeks.

'You idiot,' she said in a husky, tight voice and pushed her hair back from her face before going to take the shower she had come up for.

And she tried to persuade herself that it was shock. For if she weakened towards Rafe she would never be free of him. He was an arrogant despot, and the sooner she left Te Puriri the better it would be for everyone. But first—first she had to find some way to make it impossible for Melly to marry Derek.

Beneath the sharp darts of warm water she revolved plans and plots in her brain before realising that she really only had two chances. Either she convinced Melly that Derek was still hankering after his ex-wife, or she pushed Derek until he slid over the edge into the violence that seemed an integral part of his character. Both seemed impossible.

So why didn't she just tell Rafe? His shoulders were broad enough, he would know how to handle the situation.

Oh, let's be truthful, she told herself savagely. You won't tell Rafe because you still think Derek had a good reason for hitting you. You think it was your fault, and the reason why you think it was your fault is that you were in love with Rafe when you married

Derek and you are in love with him now and you think that if you tell Rafe he will blame you too.

'You are too screwed up to be true,' she said aloud, turning the water off with a vicious twist of her wrist.

As she dragged the towel over her cringing flesh she berated herself for her convoluted thinking.

'But I can't,' she whispered at last, mopping up tears which threatened to overflow her eyes. 'I just *can't*. I love him so and he feels something pretty powerful for me, but we're both prisoners of the past. If I told him about Derek he probably wouldn't believe me, but if he did he'd despise me.'

Even as she said it she knew that she was wrong, but the taboo against revealing her experience was so strong that she could not bring herself to do it. Why? *Why* did she still cringe at the thought of anyone else knowing?

It was she who had been beaten, she who had suffered, she who should hold the whip hand. Even the clichés, she thought sombrely, dealt in images of pain and servitude. *Whip hand!* Shivering, suddenly cold, she recalled the knowing look in Derek's eyes whenever he saw her. Somehow he was still able to impress his will on her in spite of his wariness. Oh, he was afraid of her and what she might do, but whenever he saw her he felt dominant. There was a horrible, a frightening, intimacy between them, a bond based on her past terror.

What could be easier than to go to Rafe and say, 'Rafe, I came back because when we were married Derek beat me, on occasions quite severely, and a psychiatrist I saw a week ago said that he'll probably beat Melly too.'

As she climbed, shivering between the sheets she imagined the scene, saw it all in her mind's eye, but she knew that she would not do it, and calling herself a coward, despising herself for it, did not make any difference.

Her heavy lashes flicked then slid slowly down to

cover the turbulent green of her eyes. Dreamily she
imagined Rafe telling her that she was not to worry,
that nobody would ever hurt her again, that he would
take care of her. It could never happen, but dreams
were free.

How did she know that he would never use
violence against her? The capacity for violence was in
him; she recognised it, always had. Yet she had never
feared him.

Sleepily she decided that it was because of his
immense willpower. And because she recognised that
for him, his capacity to hurt was allied to a fierce
protectiveness for anything weaker than himself. Rafe
could be tender, even gentle, with those he loved. With
Melly, with a dog he had owned when he was young—
on occasion, she remembered, even with the stepsister
he mistrusted so. When she was hurt, and a few times
when she had emerged from her shell to reveal that she
was upset, he had been kind, even if it was an
impersonal kindness. He was a good boss, too,
demanding yet fair. The men at Te Puriri respected him
but they liked him too. Hard but just, she thought
wearily.

She was asleep when he came in but she reacted to his
presence as she always did, as she always would. Slowly
her lashes lifted; they were wet, she realised, and the
sobbing which had been part of her dream was her own.

'Go away,' she commanded, only the words made no
sound and when he came to stand by the bed she turned
over on to her side and hid her face in the pillow,
cursing whatever ill-fortune that had led him to pass her
room just then.

The side of the bed sank as he sat down. He made no
attempt to touch her, but after a moment he said
quietly, 'I'm sorry. I had no right to abuse you the way
I did.' She didn't respond and he went on, 'When I saw
the engine in flames and realised that it was you in the

cab I—well, I thought that I was going to have to watch you burn to death.'

Incredibly his voice faltered.

'I'd have thought you'd be glad,' she said waspishily, fighting her instinct to give in to him.

'I deserved that, I suppose.'

'No,' she sighed, turning her head on the pillow, 'I'm sorry. That was a rotten thing to say.'

'I don't blame you. How are you now? No burns?'

'No. My hands are a bit sore where I landed on them in the gravel but——'

'Let me see.'

She made no attempt to show him, so he turned her gently, smiling rather ironically as she kept them firmly under the covers.

'Show me,' he insisted. 'Or do you want me to find them for myself?'

He had only to look at her like that, eyes narrowed, mouth slightly quirked, and every nerve in her body sang into life.

Slowly she lifted her arms, keeping the sheet in place with her elbows. He examined the pink palms carefully, his expression grave if you could discount the tiny glittering points of fire in the darkness of his gaze. Jennet couldn't. Strange pins and needles were stabbing under her skin and she tried to tug her hands away. He tightened his grip, not painfully but with the determination which was such an important part of his character.

'They're all right,' she said swiftly. 'I found some stuff in the medicine cabinet to put on them.'

'Good,' he said absently. His mouth had tightened but he wasn't angry. He was watching a tiny pulse in her throat as it throbbed like a wild thing caught in a net. 'Why do we fight?' he asked.

Her shoulders lifted. 'Personality clash?'

It was a flippant little suggestion, but she was

frightened. When he was behaving like a tyrant she could hold her own against him but like this he disarmed her entirely.

'You don't believe that.'

Her tongue touched the centre of her top lip for a moment. 'No?' she said, the word hard and flat with control. 'What then?'

'This, I think,' he told her quite gently as his hands slipped from hers up her arms to slide beneath her back and pull her from the safe haven of her bed into his embrace. 'This,' he said as his mouth covered that betraying flicker in the soft length of her throat, 'and this . . . and this . . . and this . . .'

She melted like warmed wax into him, one hand clutching the thin material of his shirt, the other curving around his head as her fingers slid into his black hair. The shock of his mouth against her throat sent her spinning into some other plane, a dizzying world where the only reality was him—and her incandescent response.

She retained only enough sanity to moan helplessly, 'Oh—no . . .'

'Oh yes, I think so,' he muttered as his mouth quested across the smooth skin of her shoulder.

The sheet had slipped and she was naked to the waist, flushed and heated, the satiny contours of her body open to the fierce plundering of his eyes and his mouth and his hands.

'You are so beautiful,' he whispered as if it hurt him to speak, 'you make me ache just to think of you. When I saw you in that truck I thought—if she dies I'll spend the rest of my lfe searching for her.'

No word of love, but she knew better than to listen for one.

'Rafe,' she whispered into his throat, her longing and her hunger clogging her heart.

'I'm sick of fighting it. God knows, I've given sanity

and pride and discrimination a fair trial and they've
only brought me this craving that tears at me until I
can't sleep, can't think of anything but the need to lose
myself in you.'

The hot tumbled words fell out as though he could
not repress them, each stark syllable thick with desire's
ugly brother, lust, but as they had died away his mouth
was urgently searching the full curve of her breast and
she stiffened in anticipation, her breath choking in her
throat.

When at last his lips reached their destination she
groaned harshly, swamped by desire, her body
clenched. Her hands slipped beneath the material of his
shirt to cling across the hard warm strength of his back.

He made a short, urgent sound in his throat and
lowered her on to the pillows, following her down so
that she felt his weight. Her head fell back; she said
something, she never knew what, and her legs and the
lower part of her body moved in convulsive involuntary
invitation, rising to meet him so that for long moments
they lay clamped together with only the sheet and his
clothes between them.

'Yes,' he said, lifting his head from her breast to
survey the glazed passion in her face. 'Yes.'

Dark colour suffused his skin. His heavy-lidded eyes
were feverish, the black depths flaming with passion.
She welcomed the smothering intensity of his kiss,
straining to meet and match it, her body shaking with
the kind of untrammelled, uncontrolled passion only he
knew how to arouse. And only he could assuage the
desperate need in her.

As he plumbed the depths of her mouth her hands
groped down his back to his hips and held him there
while she writhed beneath his fierce masculinity.

And then Melly's voice called something outside and
they heard a quick question and answer from her to
Joy. Rafe lifted his head and said something so explicit

that Jennet's suddenly pale skin was flushed with colour.

'Will nothing go right for us?' he said savagely, frustration hardening his features as he stared down into her dazed face. Urgently, as he rolled off the edge of the bed and stood tucking his shirt back into his trousers, he said, 'Tonight, Jennet? Let me come to you tonight.'

She began to shake her head even before she had formulated the words.

'Why?' he asked softly, silkily, his expression black.

'Because——' She hesitated. Melly's feet were running quickly up the stairs. 'Because it wouldn't be wise,' she evaded while her whole body was tormented by the same frustration which sharpened his angular features.

He stared at her as though he had never seen her before and then he cursed, the obscenity ugly and jarring in the quiet room where only seconds ago there had been nothing but the wild pagan need to give—and take.

'I should have known,' he said with vicious emphasis. 'God, will I never learn?'

Diana again. Always it was Diana who came between them.

He reached the door just as Melly pushed it open from the other side. 'Out!' he said, the one biting word enough to stop her in her tracks.

For a second Melly's astounded eyes met Jennet's then she turned and walked away.

'Rafe,' Jennet said imploringly.

'Shut up.'

But she couldn't let him go like that.

'Rafe, *please*, won't you listen——'

'No. Get yourself packed. I'll put you on the plane for Auckland this afternoon.'

She drew a deep, ragged breath. 'I'm not going,' she

said, her eyes fixed on the width of his shoulders, the proudly poised head.

'You are, if I have to bind and gag you.'

'I won't go.'

He swung around and stared at her, small in the large bed, the sheet hauled high around her neck.

'What do you want?' he asked, once more in control of himself. His voice was calm, toneless, but his eyes, glinting like dark jewels, gave him away.

'I'll go after the Mialls' party,' she said desperately.

He lifted his brows. 'And will you sleep with me tonight?'

Very slowly she shook her head. He would never know how much effort it took to make the muscles move but she did it. 'Are you making that a condition?' she said, knowing that it would further anger him.

'I think you know me a little better than that. Very well then, you can stay until after the party. But I'll be watching you.'

As a threat it could not have been bettered. The cold assurance in his voice made her shiver, but although she lay with closed eyes for almost an hour, she refused to allow her brain to mull over her problems. Instead she ran through Juliet's lines, re-enacting the play in her brain until she had regained some sort of composure.

She did not expect to see Derek that day but he arrived in the afternoon, sleek, amused and arrogant. It was part of no one's plan to leave them alone together but Melly was called away to the telephone.

Derek waited until she had gone before saying insolently, 'I see you haven't managed to convince Melly to believe your lies.'

'Haven't tried,' Jennet said cheerfully.

'Why don't you give up?' He smiled, confident enough to look smug, his blond head bent in taunting commiseration. 'Melly thinks you want me back. She's always been rather jealous of you, you know. She

knows that she hasn't got that certain something you
and Diana have, so you can't blame her for being rather
pleased that I'm in love with her now, and not you. Or
for suspecting that perhaps you're regretting your dash
for freedom.'

It sounded dreadfully reasonable, even if Derek
simplified Melly's character. After all, Melly had
basked in her parents' love; she had no cause to be
jealous of Jennet.

She returned his smile, lowering her lashes in a
provocative sweep.

'I think you're wrong,' she murmured and ran her
tongue along her bottom lip. 'Still, I'm beginning to
wonder if I didn't come back on a wild goose chase.
Melly seems quite capable of looking after herself. And
Rafe is here to look after her too.'

'Then you're going?'

He realised his mistake immediately. From beneath
her lashes Jennet saw his quickly hidden chagrin. Derek
firmly believed in the superiority of the male sex.
Experience had taught him that women were stupid
creatures, easily dazzled by charm and a handsome
face. It would be silly for Jennet to put him on guard.

So she laughed, deep and warm in her throat, and
retorted, 'Don't be silly. Rafe and I are only just getting
to know each other again.'

He hated that. The shallow blue eyes became sullen
as he said through gritted teeth, 'Perhaps I should tell
him that you're as frigid as an iceberg.'

'I'm not,' she taunted, moving away. 'After I left you
I soon discovered the reason for my lack of response to
your lovemaking. No other man has ever complained. I
wonder if you'll call Melly frigid?'

By now she was walking towards the door, but even
with her back to him she could feel the anger she had
courted.

It still came as a shock when he jerked her around to

face him. He was white, the muscles in his face working
as he swore, 'You lying little whore! By God, I'll——'

Jennet did not resist when his mouth crushed hers
beneath it although instant revulsion chilled her blood.
He used his superior strength to hurt her, grinding her
lips against her tightly clamped teeth, his fingers biting
into the soft flesh of her upper arms. With a sick horror
she realised that he was aroused, but before she had
time to deal with the situation voices in the hall
compelled him to push her away. Breathing heavily he
stood glaring down into her defiant face, his hands
curled at his sides, his shoulders hunched like a
predatory bird.

'Smile,' she said lightly through sore lips. 'Big brother
is on the way and you wouldn't want him to realise that
you can't keep your hands off me, would you?'

The rigidity left his body. Colour seeped back into his
skin and he jeered, 'Had you going there for a minute,
didn't I, darling?'

The opening of the door stopped her from replying.
As she swung to face Rafe, Jennet met his stony
expression with lifted chin and hard eyes.

He said something, his eyes lingering on the swollen
contours of her mouth before lifting with coldly
satirical force to hold her gaze captive.

Her smile was meaningless. She made some excuse
and went out into the hall, standing with her arms
hanging limply by her side while she stared at the
magnificent landscape on the wall opposite. Dimly she
heard Melly's voice, still talking into the telephone. The
ticking of the grandfather clock resounded loudly, each
short deliberate sound reverberating through her head.

I'm going to be sick, she thought as beads of sweat
sprang out all over her clammy skin. She couldn't
move. Even the sound of the door behind couldn't free
her.

'Wrapped in ecstasy?' Rafe's sneering voice enquired.

She swayed slightly as he came up behind her.

'Are you all right?'

Shivering, realising that she couldn't let him see her like this, she nodded, but he turned her, and when he saw her face he said something short and nasty beneath his breath and slung an arm like steel around her shoulders, urging her towards the small powder room along the hall.

The debilitating nausea faded. Faintly she said, 'No, it's all right, Rafe. I just need a drink of water.'

'Can you make it to the kitchen?'

At her nod he half carried her until they reached the big room. Blessedly, it was empty. Rafe deposited her on to one of the chairs at the table and ran water into a glass.

The swish of the liquid refreshed her. She sighed and rubbed her hand wearily across her brow, keeping her lashes lowered.

'Here.'

Her hand was remarkably steady as she took the glass, but because he just stood looming over her and didn't go away it shook as she tried to transfer it to her mouth, slopping a few drops on to the table.

'Oh, for heaven's sake.' Rafe sounded beyond exasperation, but his hand was remarkably gentle as it enclosed hers, guiding the glass to her mouth.

The water flowed smoothly down her throat. Until then she hadn't realised how parched her mouth was.

She shook her head and he withdrew the glass, setting it down on to the table. 'Well,' he drawled, tipping her chin, 'you look less like a cheese and more like a human being. He must have a powerful effect on you.'

The tip of one lean finger traced out the contours of her mouth. A little frisson of excitement raced up her spine. She kept her gaze adamantly fixed on the buckle of his leather belt, refusing to lift her lashes.

'I suppose I should be thankful that my kisses don't

produce the same response,' he went on, almost thoughtfully.

He was too astute not to have seen just how hateful Derek's embrace had been. If he told Melly that she had no need to worry about Jennet's effect on Derek then the only plan that Jennet had been able to formulate would be ruined. Melly's conviction that Jennet was a threat had to be strengthened, reinforced by every means possible.

So Jennet forced herself to smile languuorously, a slow, feline smile and lifted her lashes so that her eyes gleamed seductively. 'How do you know?' she said sweetly. 'Actually I haven't been feeling at all well since I got up this morning. I hope I haven't given Derek a bug. He'll never forgive me.'

Silence stretched out between them, tense, unbroken by any expression of the emotions which swirled through Jennet, yet coloured by both her feelings and those Rafe was controlling. Neither gave quarter. His eyes drilled into her soul and her only protection was that foolish, sleepy smile she had perfected over the years to convince television audiences that she was a siren, a man-hunting seductress.

It became painful, a meaningless grimace, but still her lips curved and her eyes beckoned because she did not know what else to do.

At last he said relentlessly, 'If you hurt Melly I'll see to it that you never have a moment's happiness or peace again in this world.'

Such menace to be contained in a few words delivered in a voice barely above a whisper! Her mouth was parched, but she dared not give herself away by finishing the water he had brought her.

'And how,' she asked, rather proud of herself because her voice was steady, 'would you do that?'

His eyes narrowed. 'Why, marry you, of course,' he said and turned and went out of the kitchen.

CHAPTER SEVEN

A superb exit, she thought shakily, draining the water from the glass. Delivered with superb timing and intonation—everything perfect including the lean-hipped walk out of the room.

If she thought of it as a piece of magnificent theatre perhaps it wouldn't frighten her so much. He had threatened her before and she hadn't been cowed, so why was this any different? He must know that there was no way he could force her to marry him.

I'd sooner play water-polo with a shark, she thought. It would be about the same danger risk. Marriage to Derek had been hell, but marriage to Rafe would be hell with the Devil's personal supervision.

And she had better push it to the back of her mind now for it was not going to help her achieve her aim. On the other hand, the fact that Derek could still be made to want her might. The memory of his greedy mouth made her give a fastidious little shudder, but she forced herself to assess as cold-bloodedly as she could, just how, if she had to, she would use his weakness.

It would be the first time she had ever consciously and deliberately used her sexuality to manipulate a man and the thought of it made her stomach twist in a spasm, but she was a realist. In this kind of war she would have to use the few weapons she had and one of them was the disturbing collection of physical attributes which made men look at her with lust.

She got to her feet, carried the glass over to the sink and washed and dried it. When the kitchen had been remodelled, Joy, or whoever had made the decisions, had kept to the conventional concept so there was a window above the sink. It looked out over a lawn and the kitchen garden, a long border against a rock wall in which grew every herb Joy could track down as well as clusters of wallflowers and bulbs and an assortment of small shrubs, several in flower. A fantail was flitting swiftly from twig to twig, catching small unseen insects in its beak.

Behind the wall was the orchard where two almond trees robed in the palest of pinks were an intimation of fairyland. Two peach trees beyond them again held boughs of slightly deeper pink up to the sky. They must, Jennet thought, ripen well before Christmas. Tamarillo trees sheltered the exotic egg-shaped fruit, ruby-red or yellow with enormous leaves and behind them were other fruit trees, still bare and leafless.

The orchard had always been an enchanted place to Jennet. She remembered long summer days when the best shade was beneath one of the three huge avocados planted many years ago by Rafe's grandmother. In winter daffodils and jonquils bloomed in a scented carpet beneath the trees, in the autumn belladonna lilies lifted their naked pink and carmine and white trumpets. Immense hedges of Japanese cedars cut the orchard off from the station. The wall on the fourth side was pierced by a little wicket gate. The only other entrance was the farm gate used by the tractor which did the heavy work there.

Perhaps because of this she had always thought of it as a secret place, magical, not quite of this world. Before she had discovered her own little dell she had spent much of her time in the orchard.

Now she walked out across the kitchen garden to the wicket gate. One of the farm cats, a large unctuous creature with serrated ears above a smug black face, stretched its back and claws beneath a daphne bush then padded lazily after her.

Once in the shelter of the hedges the sun beat down

with unremitting force. The five sheep who kept the pasture short lifted their heads and eyed Jennet and her attendant with mild curiosity before resuming their life's most important work. A single strand of electrified wire kept them from the citrus orchard. It was sheep height so Jennet was able to step over it. The cat knew what it was, too. Jennet smiled as he lowered his tail carefully before strolling under it.

Lemons and lemonades glowed like oval suns, the mandarins were small and vivid against their glossy green leaves.

'Now, which mandarins peel the easiest?' Jennet asked her companion. 'Clementines or Satsumas or Karas? I wonder.'

'Satsumas,' Rafe said, so close behind her that she jumped and turned to face him, her expression protesting.

'I wish you wouldn't do that,' she objected, not trusting him an inch.

He wore that arrogant, high-handed look of his, that 'lord of all creation and answerable to none' expression she and Melly had used to call it, and the smile on his well-shaped mouth was neither amused nor pleasant.

'Well, help yourself,' he said. 'We don't charge for them.'

'What are you doing here?'

He picked a mandarin, strong fingers working swiftly as he peeled off the golden skin and threw it under the tree.

'Here,' he said softly. 'Come and get it.'

She shook her head. It was incredible but she was frightened. This beautiful place, in broad daylight and yet she was afraid.

'All right then,' he said, apparently bored, and halved the tiny fruit, offering her a portion while he ate his share in two mouthfuls.

Reluctantly Jennet stretched out her hand and was

instantly caught and pulled to him.

'Rafe . . .' she objected.

'Open your mouth,' he said with infuriating coolness.

From beneath her lashes she saw nothing but a kind of lazy impassivity in his face yet his grip on her was too firm to make any effort to break free. Slowly she obeyed and a segment of satsuma was placed on her tongue.

When the sharp, sweet morsel was gone, he fed her another and another until he said, 'My finger is sticky,' and placed it against her lips.

Slowly, impelled by some instinct she should have ignored, Jennet's tongue curved on to his finger, working slowly around it so that the juice of the mandarin was removed.

Her lashes flickered. She could feel a familiar pressure in her throat, in her breasts, a familiar hunger in the pit of her stomach. Looking up into the ruthless face above her she was sixteen again. She remembered then the first sharp pangs of desire as if fountained through blood and sinews and nerves, igniting her, forcing her now to recognise a bitter and painful truth.

Only this man, she thought bemusedly. It had never been like this since, not with Derek, not with anyone. There had never been this conviction of absolute rightness, of—fulfilment.

What was between them was love. Passion and hatred and suspicion—and love. She should have realised much sooner. Derek had seen it. And although Rafe would never admit it, he too must know, for that was why he had to hate her. She was dangerous, a threat to that splendid self-sufficiency of his.

'You look like a wary cat,' he said softly and closed her eyes with kisses before his warm, demanding mouth moved to her temple.

Almost soothed by the persuasive touch of his lips she leaned into him, a soft sigh escaping through lips which stung with the need for his lovemaking.

They stayed locked together, his arms confining her with her cheek resting against the hard curve of his shoulder. The sun beat down on Jennet's face; in a daze of happiness she felt his mouth in her hair.

'Pretty little thing,' he said lazily.

'Don't be condescending.'

She could hear his smile. 'Beautiful, then. The kind of beauty which cuts through the civilised ethos we aspire to. Just to look at you is to want you.'

Not everyone, she wanted to tell him. Not every man, although many mistook her beauty for the woman beneath it, treating her as an object not a living, intelligent person.

But all she said, inadequately, was, 'It isn't always pleasant.'

'No, I suppose not, although men have conspired together over the years to make it seem the ultimate perfection. The mask is mistaken for the person. I know how that feels.'

Surprised into an unguarded little movement, she said nothing, but she felt his noiseless chuckle, before he continued, 'Women do it, too. They don't demand beauty but—more tangible assets. Money, security. If I came to you tomorrow and told you that it had all gone, that I had nothing but my bare hands and my brain, what would you do?'

It was heaven to stand like this, resting so confidingly against him and listening to him talking to her, for once with the tense, power-seeking cut and thrust of their usual conversation absent.

'Offer you bed and board and whatever else I could give,' she said, adding shyly, 'not that you'd ever come to me.'

'Just like that, no strings, no conditions? I find that hard to believe.' He sounded cynical beyond belief but strangely, there was no bitterness in the deep voice.

Yet the words were like small destructive blows to her body.

'Modesty sits rather oddly on your shoulders, Rafe. If you really think that your material assets are the only reason you attract women you must need your head read.'

'No, not the only reason, but certainly the main one.'

She laughed at that, the warm delightful sound tinged with some mischief, tilting her head so that she looked up into his dark, shuttered face. 'Darling, you're priceless. You're a very handsomely packaged piece of masculinity, you know, although that's not your main attraction. Derek is almost as good looking as you, but he doesn't have to swat adoring females off like flies. No, with you it's that combination of contained strength, the hint of austerity and the total and complete authority that gets us.'

He grinned, mocking her. 'Go on, you fascinate me. Have you ever thought of using that creative streak of yours? Writing plays?'

'No, I mean it.' She lifted her finger and traced the strong harsh line of his jaw, feeling the skin tighten beneath her touch. A kind of languor made her boneless, careless of consequences. The clamour in her body had eased into a brilliant awareness. Her discovery of the love she had carried in her heart for years, had liberated her from the tension she always felt in his presence. Now that she no longer had to hide from herself she could relax.

'Women can't resist self-sufficiency,' she told him solemnly, her eyes sparkling with laughter. 'We have to be needed, wanted, to make a man feel that he isn't complete without us. It's an old atavistic notion, almost an instinct, implanted in our genes. And then there's that intriguing combination of virility and austerity. Aha, we say, a sensual Puritan and our mind thrills to all sorts of delicious, forbidden thoughts.'

He was laughing openly at her now but his mouth straightened, and he asked, 'And the authority?'

'Well, we're programmed to seek security,' she returned with a limpid look. 'You see, in spite of feminism and the twentieth century and plain common sense which tells us there's no such thing as complete security, tucked away in every woman is this instinct which tells her that she should be looking around for a man to protect her and the babies from the local sabre-toothed tiger and woolly mammoth. An intelligent courageous man, preferably big.' Here she ran an exploratory hand from his elbow to his shoulder, enjoying the automatic tensing of muscle and skin before giving him a dazzling smile.

The nonsense helped her control the rising tide of hunger in her body. It also summoned that rare, wolfish smile as a response.

'As it happens,' he told her, 'woolly mammoths were vegetarians. I think they lived on buttercups and grass. But I see what you mean.'

'I thought you might.'

'Hasn't it occurred to that instinct that big men need a lot of food to keep them going? Food taken from the mouths of those babies?'

'Oh, I don't think instincts can reason,' she said, tilting her head to one side in mock thoughtfulness.

Again that slashing grin. 'So I've been right all these years in assuming that it was my bank balance which attracted women.'

'Partly,' she sighed in sympathetic tones. A mischievous glint transformed her eyes into green jewels, exotic, provocative. 'At least, the security it evokes. But you see it's not our fault, either. I mean, who can escape heredity?'

'Who indeed?' For a moment the angular features hardened. 'Why even try?' he muttered as his head lowered and his mouth took hers.

This time, freed from the fear of understanding her emotions, she allowed herself the freedom to respond fully. It seemed right that he should make a strange choked little noise in his throat before, without breaking the kiss, he stepped backwards so that he was leaning against the bole of the flowering peach. His arms tightened, pulling her against his body into intimate contact. As Derek had been earlier, he was aroused, but she wanted this, she felt no shred of distaste, willingly pressing herself against him so that her soft form was lying open to him.

His mouth was not hurtful as Derek's had been. It was gentle, but determined, seducingly sweet, summoning such intense excitement that she was overcome by it, she didn't know how to cope and she went under completely.

Only dimly was she aware of the hand that slid up to fondle the smooth skin of her back, and discover that she wasn't wearing anything underneath the prim shirt.

Beneath her fingers his skin was hot and damp, silk over steel, incredibly exciting.

Then he said something and she whispered his name, turning her face into his neck, her tongue flicking out in tiny involuntary movements to caress the salty skin.

Strange to feel a strong man flinch at such a tiny caress. Strange to feel that hard body quicken against her, his hands slide together down behind the waistband of her slacks and pull her with a swift, violent ferocity against him so that she gasped and cried out, for his need and passion sent a primitive hunger coursing through every cell in her body.

Like calling to like, she thought dazedly, holding on to his shoulders as if she was drowning. There was no tenderness, no respect in this embrace, nothing but a current of elemental fire which leapt from one to the other, ignited and fed by the abandoned response each advance met.

He was speaking, his head bent so that his mouth was by her ear, blocking out the dazzling warmth of the sun.

'What?' she said vaguely, turning her head to meet his. Her mouth searched blindly for his, found it, but he lifted his head away from her and spoke again and this time the words impinged.

'Is this how your ex-husband makes you feel?'

And while she was still trying to make sense of the pattern of words he repeated it in a voice dead and devoid of emotion.

Slowly, like a woman in the grip of a nightmare, she awoke to her actions—and his. Held in that grip, his hands cruel on her hipbones, able to feel every inch of his body and its wild response from the heavy lifting movements of his chest to the taut length of his thighs, she knew that he wanted her and that yet again he had rejected her.

And it had been so easy; he had proceeded exactly as he had that first time, lulled her into acceptance with his usually relaxed attitude, a little conversation and then the soundless cruel swoop to the kill.

And like the hawk's prey, she had been taken by something she hadn't even recognised.

She welcomed the anger which rode like a flood through her body, for it hid the shame and the persistent, wounding pain, but she forced herself to relax. The evidences of his arousal were fading. That cold, remorseless brain was once more in control.

So she said as calmly as she could above the painful slamming of her heart, 'Not quite, darling, but then Derek is not quite so experienced as you—or so well-equipped by nature.'

Her only protection was that small one afforded by her eyelids. She kept them resolutely lowered to hide the betrayed confusion in her eyes.

'Oh?' The syllable was drawled out with derisive

mockery. 'Has your instinct discarded him as not suitable material to take on a marauding cave bear?'

She couldn't manage a smile, but at least her voice had a note of lilting amusement in it when she replied, 'Experience, my sweet. Instinct can be overriden by experience. Derek does very well, but he hasn't that basic ruthlessness which you possess.'

'And that's what turns you on?'

'Either that or your money,' she said flippantly and made to pull away.

It was a mistake. His hands tightened and he chuckled softly as he lifted her, holding her so that her face was on a level with his. Startled, her lashes flew up, and her glance was caught and held by the obsidian darkness of his, opaque with warning and a cruel enjoyment of her situation.

'So keep out of his bed,' he said quietly.

Shrugging, she leaned forward and kissed the brutal, beautiful line of his mouth, reacting to his involuntary response with a knowing smile. Against his lips she said, 'I'll do what I want to, when I want to, with whom I want to, and there's nothing you can do about it, *dear, kind, noble* Rafe.' Her warm voice laughed over the adjectives, deliberately taunting.

To punish him a little further she hooked her legs around his, felt his desire surge through his body for a second and was ready, waiting, when he dropped her, the dark, autocratic lines of his face harsh and contemptuous.

He swore while she tucked her shirt back into her jeans, the imprecations heavy on the dancing air until she taunted, 'Oh, don't be so stupid, Rafe. You deserve to be punished a little. What you did was hardly Queensberry rules, was it?'

'No,' he said, and suddenly the anger was damped down, controlled as he finished, 'but it did show that I can get you into my bed any time I like to try.'

'Oh no,' she said, smiling, shaking her head so that several pink petals drifted from the soft, gleaming tresses, 'sorry, darling, you've just queered your pitch. Not now, not ever.'

'I never could resist a challenge,' he murmured reaching for her.

His mouth was just as seducingly sweet, her response as exciting, but Jennet stood in his grasp without moving. She didn't even close her eyes, noting with detached interest that when he kissed he kept his open, too. Probably, she thought knowledgeably, because it might be seen as a sign of vulnerability, a kind of symbolic placing of oneself in the partner's power. And Rafe was far too self-sufficient to do that. Far too cold, far too arrogant. Far too cruel.

And she loved him, had always loved him in spite of the instinct of self-preservation which had tried to hide the truth from her for so many years. Loving Rafe could only mean more pain, more humiliation, a constant aching rent in the fabric of her personality.

At last he released her, saying with merciless precision, 'You can turn it off and on like a——'

'Oh, why hesitate? Like a whore, I feel sure you were going to say.' It hurt, every breath, every beat of her heart, every movement of her body hurt, as if she had been tortured for weeks, years, but she had come a long way from the shy adolescent who had been so lacking in confidence. She stood straight as a wand, her eyes meeting his in cool challenge.

'Very well, then, like a whore.' He was watching her, perhaps wondering what was going on behind the beautiful empty mask of her face. Cruelly, deliberately, he continued, 'But you're little better than that, are you? You sell your body. The only difference is that instead of honestly giving it in return for the money, you make men pay for the shadow, for fodder for their fantasies. Except when you play Juliet, of course.'

'Oh, of course,' she murmured. 'Shakespeare is sacred, we all know that.'

She could bear no more. A little clumsily she turned away, but stopped the moment his hand touched her shoulder.

'Yes?' she asked, the word dipped in ice.

'Just remember, Jennet. If I see you near Derek again I'll take what you so blatantly offered me a few minutes ago. Even if you manage to keep up the masquerade of resistance.'

'But that would be rape,' she said silkily.

She could hear the cynical smile in his voice. 'No, my darling. I wouldn't rape you. Ever.' The voice lowered, became husky, promising, tormenting. 'By the time I've finished with you you'll be begging me to take you. If you think—well, there are forms of degradation even you have probably never heard of.'

As she walked away through the smiling day Jennet found herself insisting wearily that he had made an empty threat, while the hair on the back of her neck refused to lie down and she knew she was trying to fool herself. There had been a note of implacable decision in those last sentences which terrified her.

She thought once more of telling him about her marriage. Up in her bedroom, surrounded by the paraphernalia of her childhood, she sat on the bed, hands clasped between her knees and stared at her feet.

How would she do it? Rafe, I don't think Melly should marry Derek because ... and then launch into her shaming little story, for in spite of the best efforts of the psychiatrist she still felt shamed by it.

Only now she knew why. Because for all her righteous indignation, Derek had been quite correct when he blamed her complete lack of response to him on her unacknowledged, repressed desire for Rafe.

So far she had accomplished nothing. Nothing at all. Melly was still determined to marry Derek, still

convinced that her sister had come back to cause
trouble, and for no other reason. Derek had been too
clever for her. Every time their eyes met she saw his
triumph and had to stem her own despairing
helplessness. The only plan her mind had come up with
was acutely dangerous, now that Rafe had taken a hand
in the affair.

Shivering, her skin taut, she stood up. She would
have to persuade Melly that she spoke the truth and if
she failed then she would stake everything on her
decision to force Derek's hand.

And if that failed, she thought desperately, she would
have no choice but to tell Rafe everything. He would
not believe her but the revelation might make him keep
a close watch on Melly. He would see to it that she was
not left alone and helpless, caught in the same trap that
Jennet had been caught in.

That done, Rafe warned, she would go back and pick
up the threads of her life.

For there was no future for her at Te Puriri. Oh, she
could become Rafe's mistress. He wanted her. If she
surrendered, made it obvious that she would take him
on his terms, he'd enjoy her. For a few weeks, perhaps a
few months. And she would be happy for those weeks
or months. Her love, that obsessional ardour which had
lasted for so many years, would pave the way for
another, more final, rejection.

But even as she thought of it, she knew she would not
do it. If she let him, Rafe could cripple her.

We are all scarred, she thought, sombrely, our souls
marked by ghosts.

Dinner was eaten rather hurriedly. Rafe had a
meeting and Melly was going to see a friend who had
just come home from a holiday in South America. Left
to her own devices Jennet tried to read a book subtitled
Civilisation and Capitalism, 15th–18th Centuries, before
exchanging it for an amusing romp by Georgette Heyer.

Neither made any impression on her. When she looked down at her hand she was alarmed to see it trembling.

Wearily, she decided to see if she could sleep. The house was very quiet, its welcoming ambience never more soothing.

Halfway to the stairs she leaned against the wall, staring with blank eyes through the carved wooden arch with its classically capped pillars to a niche painted in *trompe l'oeil*. She had read somewhere that the Hollingworth who had built the homestead had imported Italian workmen. Perhaps one of them had painted the exquisite little scene, a marble balustrade overhung with vines and beyond that a garden, classical with cypresses and a fountain. Even after all these years the colours were soft and fresh, the little landscape as deceptive to the vision as it had been meant to be.

'Oh, *God*,' Jennet whispered, swamped by an aching sense of loss and desolation. With one last look she fled, racing up the stairs to the refuge of her room.

But she could not settle, Her thoughts, her attempts to deal with her emotions, had her pacing restlessly back and forth, until finally she pulled a jacket from the wardrobe and ran quietly down the stairs and out on to the terrace in front of the house.

Although chilly, the night was one of those magnificent spectacles turned on by winter. No wind, the moon not yet up, just the black sky of infinity and the blaze of the stars, incredibly close and clear, the Milky Way, a ragged swathe of diamond dust from one horizon to the other, the closer stars glittering in their magnificent chaste remoteness.

Walking slowly, quietly except for the soft sound of her shoes on the stones, she found the winter constellations with their euphonious names, Scorpio, Aquila, Saggitarius. And although bright Canopus and Sirius, the most dazzling of all the stars, had dipped below the horizon, there was the little Southern Crown and the two brilliant pointers to the Southern Cross to take their place, as well as blazing red Antares, sinister in the Scorpion.

Dougal had taught her the names and constellations, letting her tag along on nights when he had gone out with his binoculars to watch the skies. She shivered as she remembered him, a tired man, weary before his time, telling her to look at the stars and her own troubles would seem very small.

Perhaps they did, but at the moment even the stars couldn't make her relax. As she paced the length of the terrace, hands stuffed in the pockets of her jacket, her breath a small smoke in front of her, she tried to bring some sort of order into the events of the past weeks, to formulate some sort of plan.

Nothing happened, of course, nothing so miraculous as a new way of dealing with the situation. Yet still she paced, stopping now and then to stare for long moments up into the sky.

CHAPTER EIGHT

WHEN the lights of the car stabbed through the
darkness she was standing by one of the borders,
breathing in the fabulous scent of a bush of Japanese
honeysuckle. Without checking pace, the big vehicle
moved quietly on past the house. She heard the soft
sound of its door, the faint rustle of the garage door as
Rafe closed it.

She had not moved when he appeared beside her. No
sound had betrayed his approach yet she knew where he
was, knew that he was coming for her.

'How was the meeting?' she asked, meaningless
words.

'All talk and no action. Typical.'

'No action?'

In the bright starshine she saw his swift, flashing grin.
'Well, a little. Enough to make it worthwhile, I suppose.
What are you doing out here? Communing with ghosts?'

She was shaken again at this further evidence of his
perspicacity.

'How did you know?'

'Oh, something in the way you looked. Haunted, I
suppose.'

'We are, aren't we?' she said sadly.

He didn't pretend to misunderstand her. 'You're
doing some haunting yourself.'

'Rafe . . .'

'Yes?'

She sought for words, her face turned away from
him. Slowly, stumbling a little, the beautiful warm voice
tentative, she said, 'If I told you—if I said that I had a
good reason for coming back—would you believe me?'

'Of course I would.' He waited while she looked sharply up at him, her face a pale blur in the darkness, before continuing blandly, 'I've always known what it is. You don't want Compton to be happy.'

'No, it's not that,' she said hopelessly, pulling back.

His hands around her face were warm, almost gentle, but they held her captive. 'Revenge is not a particularly worthwhile motive, is it?' he mused as his thumb stroked across the senstitive skin of her lips. 'It is, however, one I can understand. I'm not a forgiving person myself.'

'No,' she said wearily.

He smiled, using his thumb to push aside her lips, to test the outline of her teeth in a caress which made her heart beat unevenly, crazily. Her tongue touched his skin, delicately savouring his taste and then his thumb was replaced by his mouth and she sighed and relaxed against him, searching for comfort in the most basic way.

A long time later he spoke against her throat, the words muffled but distinguishable. 'Why are we out here in the cold? My bedroom is much warmer, much more comfortable than this.'

The thread of cynical amusement in the deep tones only emphasised the raw passion there. Jennet was tempted, sorely so, for her body ached with a frustration which had become like an old friend, but she said in a remote little voice, 'Sorry, darling.'

'Jennet.'

'Mmm?'

'It's those ghosts again, isn't it?'

'You summoned them, Rafe, not me.' Her sigh tailed off into a bitter little laugh. 'It's strange, isn't it? She's not even dead.'

'No. But my father is.'

Something in the way he said it made her shiver. 'Would you—do you really wish she was dead?'

'Oh, God knows.' His arms tightened about her, crushing her, hurting her. 'If I wanted her dead then you'd have to die too, wouldn't you, and I don't think I'd like that. I have other plans for you.' And bending his dark head in the cool sweet-smelling darkness with the ageless stars wheeling above them he told her what those plans were, his voice slurring as the hot words burned across her mind and she felt the hunger and the tension in him. Felt it and responded to it, her brain at the mercy of her questing flesh while he spoke words she had never heard from a man's lips, words that were harsh with a passion too long suppressed.

'Rafe,' she muttered, shaking with the determination not to give in. 'Please listen to me.'

'I don't want to hear you talk.' He laughed soundlessly and went on, 'Deeds, not words, Jennet.'

'Please Rafe. I must tell you . . .'

He sighed, and took her hand and slid it under his jacket so that she was pressed against him, trapped by his warmth and the sensual weakness of her own desires.

'Very well, then, tell me, and after that we'll make love and the only sounds I want to hear from you will be the strange choked little noises you make when I touch you.'

She flinched but the blood was running hot through her veins and she said without hope, 'Don't you want to know why I have to stop this marriage?'

'I already know.'

'No you don't.' She was shivering but she persisted, 'Please listen to me.'

'I'll listen.'

But he wasn't going to believe her; she could tell by the bored note in his voice.

Stumbling, her voice barely audible, she said wretchedly, 'Rafe, I left Derek because he beat me.'

Silence. After a dreadful, tense few moments he

responded politely, 'I've often felt like it myself, Jennet.
I know, he told me.'

'He—*told* you?'

The broad shoulders lifted in a slight shrug. 'Last
night.'

'I see.' But she didn't.

As if she hadn't spoken, he said calmly, 'I must admit
I'd have felt murderous if I caught my wife of a few
months in bed with my cousin.'

For a few seconds she literally couldn't think. His
words went round and round her head, echoing, until at
last she managed to make sense of them. Then,
surprisingly enough, she thought with almost detached
interest that Derek had indeed been clever. To a fiercely
possessive, territorial male like Rafe, unfaithfulness
would be the unforgiveable sin.

'Is it any use telling you that I was not—that I didn't
go to bed with Trent?' she asked.

He laughed again. 'No, I'm afraid not, darling. Your
subsequent actions rather give the lie to that, don't
they? You ran away with the guy.'

It was hopeless, useless, yet still she persisted. 'Or
that Derek systematically beat me from the first?'

'Sorry,' he said, and she could tell that he was
smiling; his voice revealed a savage, contemptuous
amusement. 'Good try, though. The poor swine can't
really prove that he didn't, can he? If you'd seen him
after you left you'd know why I don't believe you. He
was, quite literally, distraught. I could have told him
you weren't worth it but you had him so tied up he
couldn't see straight.'

She couldn't bear his closeness. How could he think
so vilely of her yet hold her in his arms as if he wanted
her? But when she made to step back, his hold
tightened. He let her feel his strength as she struggled
against him, his breathing not altering until she gave up
and stood, stiff and taut in his arms.

Then he lowered his dark, proud head to rest his cheek against her forehead and said, 'But the clincher, Jennet, is the fact that you didn't complain. If Derek had made a habit of beating you you'd have done something about it, wouldn't you?'

'Come to you?' she suggested bitterly and then, before he could answer, 'you don't understand.'

'I understand too well. You married Derek because you liked having him panting with desire at your heels and because you thought he had money. He told me all about it last night. When you tired of being his wife, when you realised that Compton Downs was mortgaged up to the hilt, you did exactly what your mother did. You wanted him to sell up and get out. But he was tougher than my father and he refused. So you hopped into bed with his cousin and when Derek lost his temper with you, you ran away. Now you're intent on revenging yourself and you're not in the least choosey about the weapons you use. Only it won't work, sweetheart. We all know you for what you are, and that draws your poison before you've had a chance to strike.'

Oh, Derek had been brilliant. So skilfully playing on Rafe's prejudices, using facts to cobble together a tissue of lies which could not be disproved.

Jennet stood very still, her brain working coldly and with clear precision. Derek had always been cunning, quick to seize an advantage to manipulate people. His downfall was his conceit, that arrogance which had refused to believe that she would leave him, the same self-confidence which had made him pursue Melly when he knew that Jennet would do all in her power to prevent the wedding.

That quick confidence in his own cleverness, so at variance with Rafe's cool competence, was the only weapon she had against him. That and the fact that he still wanted her. It angered him that she was no longer in his power. Her refusal to be afraid of him, her self-assurance, hit at the basic insecurity which the whole false edifice of his personality had been erected to hide. Fundamentally Derek was weak, a bully, and he knew it, and he had given his life over to hiding it.

Jennet knew it too. She was the only other person, apart from Trent Addison, his cousin, who understood him, and although he was confident that he had made it impossible for her to harm him he was wary of her.

And that was why she was not going back to Sydney until she had seen this thing through. Somehow she must find a way of undermining that charming front he presented to the world until he stood revealed as the shoddy, unhappy person he was and Melly would be safe.

'What are you thinking?' Rafe said, shifting slightly.

Jennet tried to pull away but his hands settled her between his legs, holding her hips until she made no further resistance. She sighed again and undid his jacket, leaning into him, her cheek resting on his shirt, warm with the blood beating through his body. His hands slid in a leisurely fashion up her back; he smiled, totally confident of her capitulation.

'Tell me,' he coaxed, knowing that her body was open to his touch, that her heart was picking up speed.

'Secrets,' she said sadly.

'Always secrets in those shadowy eyes.' His breath was warm across her skin. 'Keep your secrets, darling, until you're in my bed. Then I'll have every one of them from you.'

'You don't think much of women, do you?' she said slowly, lost in a mysterious sensual world where the strength and warmth of his body and the soft, lazy movement of his mouth over her face were the only reality.

He laughed. 'I'm not a misogynist, if that's what you're thinking. But I learnt early that women aren't to be trusted.'

'Your mother died, and left you alone.'

There was a moment's silence before he said in an arrested voice, 'How astute of you, Jennet.'

His mouth had moved from the line of her cheekbone to rest on the soft hollow beneath her ear. She shivered again, common sense warned her that now was the time to stop this slow relentless seduction before it got out of hand.

'More ghosts,' she said, hardening her voice. 'There are too many of them, Rafe. And I'm slowly freezing to death.'

'Inside then.'

He didn't touch her as they walked across the wet lawn, made no effort to help her up the steps on to the terrace. She left him while he was unlocking the door, moving with no more than her usual speed up the stairs. The hall was always lit by a subdued lamp, another burned over the stairwell but the house was silent with that peculiar quietness which comes when everyone else is asleep. Jennet slipped into her room, rubbing her hands together more to convince herself that she was cold than because they were. She wasn't afraid that Rafe would follow her in. He wanted her willingly in his bed, not forced there.

Because that would give him much more satisfaction, she thought wearily. He was like the hunter who stalks his prey for the thrill of the chase. The actual kill was merely the inevitable ending to a set piece. He enjoyed this false courtship, was amused by her efforts to keep him at a distance because he was convinced that her surrender was only a matter of time.

She showered, pulled on her dressing gown and walked through the door into her room to sit down at the dressing table and brush her hair.

And for the first time in years her reflection wavered and was distorted by a film of tears.

'Oh—God,' she whispered, dropping the hairbrush to

hide her face behind her spread fingers. As the unbidden sobs forced their way into her throat she began to rock to and fro, trying to ease the pain in the physical action.

When her shoulders were caught in a grip like iron she flinched, pulling away like a stricken bird from the man behind her.

'Hush,' he said and slid his arms about her, holding her against the lean warmth of his body. 'Jennet, you'll make yourself sick. Hush, now.'

Her closed fist smeared the tears across her face but she couldn't regain control so he picked her up and sat down on the bed with her, leaning back against the headboard. Choking, gasping she burrowed into the protective strength of his body, her hands clenched on to the front of his shirt.

He said nothing more but after a few seconds his finger began to smooth the fine, soft tendrils of hair back from her wet cheeks. It moved rhythmically, sweetly, so that she felt enclosed in a cocoon of safety.

Slowly her sobs dwindled. A handkerchief appeared; she blew her nose and wiped the worst of the tears away keeping her head down so that those black eyes couldn't see the wreckage of her face. Phantom sobs made her hiccough occasionally, but she stayed where she was, afraid to move or say anything, curled up on his lap like a child. Fatigue washed over her.

After a long time he covered them both with blankets and began to slide down the bed. Jennet was almost asleep. She sighed and turned her face into his shoulder, muttering, 'Don't go.'

'No,' he said quietly.

Some time during the night she came partly awake to find herself pressed down into the mattress, lapped in warmth and peace. She smiled and slid back into sleep curving against the man who shared her bed.

He was gone when morning came, but she lay back

against the pillows and smiled again, remembering his tenderness and how secure she had felt in his arms. Surely he could not have been so gentle with her unless he felt something like affection?

Although last night's weariness had fled with last night she still suffered from the oppression of the spirits which had brought on the bout of tears. It wasn't helped by a change in the weather. Yesterday's sun had given way to a chill easterly, which whined and fretted at her windows.

Still, during the night her subconscious had come up with one suggestion. It required nerve, but she was going to ring Trent Addison. Even if he no longer felt anything for Melly it was most unlikely that he would want to see her married to Derek.

The telephone directories lived on their own shelf in the library. She would have to ring now before he went to work, because she had no idea of the name of his firm; even if she did, she might not be able to speak to him on a personal matter. Secretaries were usually very protective. A quick glance at her watch decided her. Rafe would probably be out working and with any luck Melly was still in bed. And unless Trent was a workaholic he would be at home.

At this time of the morning there was no delay; within a few minutes she was listening to the sound of the telephone ringing in Trent's house.

Almost immediately he answered, listening without comment while she explained who she was.

'I was going to ring you,' he told her crisply when she had finished. 'Brigit Miall 'phoned me last night. She told me about the engagement.'

'Are you coming?'

'Wild horses wouldn't keep me away. Have you told Melissa why you left Derek?'

She explained the situation concluding with a quick disclosure of the tale Derek had given Rafe.

'Clever bastard,' he said tightly. 'He's cut the ground out nicely from under your feet. You've not spoken to Melissa?'

'No. It didn't seem worth it. She'll believe him.'

'Hm.' Silence, then he said, 'It's a pity you didn't cite him for cruelty when you divorced him.'

'I—I couldn't,' she said weakly. 'The lawyer said it was too difficult——'

'Yes, I know. It's all right.'

'If I'd known that this was going to happen I would have.'

He said sardonically, 'If either of us had had any idea of what was going to happen I'm sure we would have acted quite differently.'

'I'm sorry,' she said tonelessly.

'My dear girl, don't be silly. I'm not blaming you for anything.' After a pause he said calmly, 'Well, I'll come up with something. If necessary I'll kidnap her.'

He meant it too. Jennet said, 'I wish I could be more helpful.'

'So do I. Still, it can't be helped. I'll see you at the party.'

'Yes. Goodbye, Trent.'

As she replaced the receiver some instinct of danger lifted the hairs on the back of her neck. Slowly her head turned to meet the peculiar glittering opacity of Rafe's gaze.

'Oh, God,' she whispered, her hand flying to her mouth.

'You lying, treacherous little slut,' he said, quite calmly, bloodless lips barely moving.

Then, as if he could not bear the sight of her he swung on his heel, leaving her to sink shakily on to a chair, her heart torn from her body.

He left Te Puriri that morning for Wellington. Something to do with the government, Melly told her. He would be back the day of the Mialls' party. So

Jennet spent the intervening days memorising her part in her next production to take her mind off the treadmill of trying to decide just how much he had heard. Her moods swung from optimistic to intensely depressed then back to optimism again.

It wasn't until the night before the party that she realised that she had given up all hope of convincing Rafe that they had some sort of future. Her hopes were pinned solely on freeing Melly.

He arrived back at Te Puriri on the afternoon plane, grim faced and with eyes which still promised retribution. Tiredness accentuated his stark bone structure but did nothing to dimish his intense, tough masculinity.

All day Jennet had been oppressed by a sense of doom, her spirits subdued by a burden which was fast becoming intolerable. Tomorrow Rafe would throw her off Te Puriri; she had accomplished nothing.

Nothing, that is, beyond falling quite desperately in love with a man who hated even the sound of her name. Every one of Rafe's prejudices had been reinforced, strengthened by her behaviour and what she couldn't help feeling were some particularly nasty tricks played by Fate. Or perhaps she was just too stupid to be able to effectively make use of the few cards she had to play.

Alone in her silent room she went listlessly across to the wardrobe. The full-length mirrors showed her a weary woman, every line of whose body proclaimed her apathy.

I am *not* going down without a fight, she told herself, forcing herself to straighten. Tonight was a night for the last throw, the determining roll of the dice in the face of fortune.

Her hands drew out a taffeta dress, black and sleek with ruffles ornamenting the camisole top and curving diagonally down the wrap-fronted skirt. Thin straps clung to her shoulders. With it she wore a wide belt of satin ribbon fastened with two silk camellias the colour of carmine. Quickly she pulled on black stockings spotted with black hailstones, thin high-heeled black shoes then sat down to brush her hair until it gleamed like blonde silk.

Her make-up was as dramatic and sensual as the dress, heavy but subtle about the eyes so that they looked like enormous sleepy green jewels and lips the exact colour of the camellias.

When all was ready she sprayed herself with *Bal à Versailles* and stood viewing her reflection in the mirror while the oriental perfume teased her nostrils. Without vanity she knew that she looked good. The tension of the past days had shadowed her eyes giving her a faintly triste appeal which was interestingly at variance with the sensual ambience she had created with clothes and cosmetics.

Absently her mind searched back over the years, recalling many of the men who had been attracted by her face and body. There had been brash men, sophisticated men, some old enough to be her father, others her own age; pleasant, unpleasant, some frightening, quite a few charming. None of them had managed to break through her defences. For years she had thought that the desperate disillusionment of her marriage had frozen her emotions. She knew better now.

When had she fallen in love with Rafe? Perhaps at the change-over from child to woman, the new-born impulses of her untutored heart and body had become fixated on him so that she could not progress beyond him. Like a colossus he had towered over her life, the only distinct figure in her memories because some time before she was sixteen she had given herself into his keeping.

The joke—bitter though it was—was that she had not even realised it. His love-making and rejection had driven her into herself and to hide the intolerable wound she had rationalised it into nothingness, striving to minimise the impact.

Her marriage had been another way of doing this. With his quick, intuitive understanding of the weaknesses of others Derek had known this and used her repressed love for another man to keep her in bondage. That was why she had stayed meekly accepting the hell he made of her life until Trent's stronger will had freed her.

But she had still been a prisoner. Now that she had accepted her emotional dependence on Rafe, and faced up to it, perhaps she would be able to escape it.

Unrequited love was not love at all. How often had she read that? Of course poets and artists and musicians refused to accept the validity of such a statement, but she must. Otherwise there was nothing ahead for her but a life as sterile as a laboratory.

Then her eye caught the tiny horse she had modelled in clay as a child and her spirits lifted. Courage flowed back through her veins. No, that was not what her life was going to be. There was her love affair with the potter's wheel and there was friendship and if she had no children of her own there were other children very much in need of love and attention. Life need never be empty; she would not be like Miss Havisham in Dicken's novel who waited in her wedding dress for the lover who jilted her, wasting her life for a phantom love and a phantom lover.

The sultry curves of Jennet's mouth tightened. Eyeing her reflection she said with a defiant lift of the chin, 'Lady, you get down there and show them you've got guts!'

They were waiting in the hall, talking in low voices. When she reached the top of the stairs Rafe and Melly both turned and looked upwards. A shiver jarred the length of her spine as she met the impact of two pairs of imperious black eyes, but imperceptibly she lifted her chin and floated down the stairs with all of the grace and arrogant confidence of a professional model, her lips pulling into a small, tantalising smile.

She felt a sudden surge of strength, her foreboding transformed into the conviction that she was going to accomplish one thing, free Melly from Derek's spell.

No, *two* things, she promised herself as Rafe's gaze moved slowly and far from subtly over her. He was never going to forget how she looked tonight. She was going to imprint her picture on to his brain so that when he was eighty he would only need to close his eyes and her image would leap into prominence, clear and sharp as she was now.

She would never know his love, never satisfy his desire, but that she would have.

'You look—lovely,' he said.

The banal little compliment gave her a pleasure that no more flowery tribute could have, because, quite literally, he could think of nothing else to say. The pinpoints of light deep in his eyes were dilated; she could sense the effort it cost him to retain control of himself.

'You look gorgeous too,' she told him generously, her eyes clinging to his. It took willpower to turn them towards Melly and drawl, 'Stunning, Mel.'

And indeed, the younger woman did look superb, the soft gold crêpe of her dress enhancing her skin so that she was a golden goddess, almost stately.

'Oh, we all look stunning,' Melly said with a snap. 'Let's go, shall we?'

CHAPTER NINE

ALTHOUGH it was quite warm the night was whipped by a brisk northerly wind which could be the harbinger of a storm. Clouds hid the moon, but its light was eerily present so that the features of the countryside could be discerned.

The journey to the Mialls' was conducted mainly in silence, but just before lifting the knocker on their door Rafe took Jennet's hand in his, enclosing it in a warm, firm, unbreakable grip. His expression defied her to object. Jennet smiled and something flickered in the depths of his eyes as his mouth hardened.

Then the door was flung open and they were welcomed inside by Brigit, very trendy in scarlet and grey. 'Come in, come in,' she urged effusively, her expression avid as her glance flashed from Melly to Rafe and thence, with a small knowing smile, to Jennet.

'Give me your wraps,' she said, masking a hint of nervousness. 'You know, you should be marketed, you three. Cloned and then sold all over the world. Every woman needs a Rafe Hollingworth, the men could have a marvellous time choosing between the sultry blonde and the raven-haired Juno.'

'What about those who prefer brunettes—or redheads?' Melly asked, failing to hide the sour note in her voice.

Brigit's gaze sharpened. Again there was that darting glance at Jennet as though they shared a secret. Jennet felt Rafe's eyes on her.

When their hostess laughed and patted his arm with a greedy little hand, he withdrew that fierce scrutiny from Jennet, smiling rather sardonically down at the older woman.

143

'Well, perhaps we'd have to provide wigs,' she said lavishly. 'We wouldn't need a wider range of men, though. You must come very close to fulfilling every woman's fantasies, Rafe.'

The fulsome compliment irritated him. Jennet could sense his withdrawal, but he was still looking acidly amused as they moved into the enormous, cathedral-ceilinged drawing-room. However when, with all of the *empressement* of a magician with a fabulous new trick, Brigit produced a tall man with dark red highlights in his hair, the amusement hardened into forbidding intolerance. His gaze, dark and deadly, transfixed Jennet.

'Look who arrived only an hour ago,' Brigit announced a little too hurriedly. 'I don't need to introduce you, do I?'

'No.' Trent Addison drawled the word with saturnine appreciation. 'I feel rather like a card from Happy Families. Or a character in *Dallas*.'

The good manners Brigit no doubt relied on, carried them through the next few minutes although tension fairly crackled in the air. To those who watched, which meant most of the twenty or so people already in the room, they must have appeared to be behaving with courtesy and restraint. After one quick glance which revealed that Derek had not yet arrived, Melly was gravely dignified, although her eyes never met those of the man beside her.

He and Rafe spoke commonplaces; Jennet was silent, conscious of Brigit's increasing nervousness.

She was, Jennet decided, realising that her love of mischief had led her into stupidity. You didn't throw the gauntlet down before Rafe Hollingworth and expect to get away with it. Not unscathed, anyway.

So, chattering in a slightly higher voice than normal Brigit swept them towards the nearest group, talking nonstop until John had poured the drinks and the doorbell summoned her away.

Some minutes later Jennet's gaze lingered on the forceful arrogant lines of Trent Addison's face as he inclined his head towards Melly, holding her attention with a hard charm which kept her captive. As if Jennet's glance was tangible he lifted his head. The heavy-lidded eyes narrowed, then he raised his glass. The silent toast was understood by them both.

A dangerous man, Jennet thought. But her ally. Any danger to her came from the man who said now, in tones as cold and implacable as the Polar snows, 'Blowing on old embers, Jennet?'

Jennet bit her lip, her eyes searching Rafe's face. He looked like a statue of an antique warrior, a fearsome barbarian who swooped down on the settled lands plundering what he desired, riches, slaves, women.

'Rafe,' she began impetuously, unable to suppress the note of pleading in her voice, 'it isn't what you think.'

'How do you know what I think? What's he like as a lover, darling?'

'Please, Rafe . . .'

He smiled and took a small mouthful of wine, waiting with what probably seemed to others to be politeness while she struggled to find the words to explain. Now was not the place, she thought, casting a swift glance around the room and the people in it, but she felt that she couldn't bear it if Rafe was going to spend the night crucifying her.

When her gaze came back to him she shivered, for his eyes glittered like black diamonds, icy, without emotion. As he lowered his wine glass, she saw a muscle pull in his jaw.

'I don't know,' she said at last, trying to convey her innocence with her voice and her face.

'Your acting ability is quite astounding,' he remarked thoughtfully, saluting her with a taunting copy of Trent's gesture with his glass. 'I feel that I should be applauding. I believe he's an excellent lover; he's certainly had enough practice.'

'He's probably very talented,' she said on a hard indrawn breath. 'He likes women, which is always a help.'

'Are you hinting that I do not?'

Her shoulders lifted in the slightest of shrugs. 'Exactly. You know, I'd never believed that our childhood affected us as strongly as Freud asserted until I thought of you. A classic case.'

He reacted to her provocation with a hard, taunting smile. 'Is that why you've spent your adult life flitting from man to man? Don't look so taken aback, I can read, you know. And your name appears frequently in the gossip columns, always with a different man. Are you trying to compensate for your mother's rejection? Or someone else's?'

Her answering smile was infinitely alluring, a teasing movement of lips as inviting as those of a siren. 'Do you really believe the sort of rubbish you read in gossip columns? You disappoint me. I'd have thought you a little more sophisticated than that.'

'God knows why one of them hasn't killed you,' he said, his smile failing to soften the menace which lurked at the back of his eyes.

'Perhaps I don't inspire such violent reactions in anyone else.'

He didn't like that. His brows twitched together and that muscle flicked again in his jaw. 'What are you insinuating?'

'I'm—nothing.' She had to back down because for a moment he had looked as though he was prepared to start a brawl, even here.

With narrowed eyes he watched as her glance slid sideways to where Melly stood with Trent at her side, his attitude stating that he had no intention of leaving her. He looked like a man who knew exactly what he wanted and was prepared to do anything to get it.

'What plot did you two hatch?' Rafe enquired silkily.

A little pale she turned her head and looked very straight at him. 'Nothing.'

'Liar.'

It hurt, but she managed to shrug. 'Believe that if you like. If you're so worried why don't you go over there and break it up?'

'It's because I'm not worried that I'm here with you,' he said caustically. 'Of the two I find you the more dangerous. Trent knows that if he hurts Melly he'll have me to deal with.'

'And don't you feel that you can deal with me?'

'Oh yes,' he said evenly, his eyes gleaming as they raked her face and her bare shoulders, lingering on the white swell of her breasts. 'If you hurt her I swear that until the day you die you'll never be able to remember tonight without a shudder. There'll never be another man for you because whenever you look at one you'll see only me and you'll be so afraid you'll ask only to live like a nun for the rest of your life.'

He spoke the threat as if it was an incantation, a sorcerer's curse. Jennet quailed at the savage purpose which rang in his voice like steel, realising that there was more here than his determination to protect Melly.

A little stir at the door caught her eye. It was Derek. Watching as he kissed Brigit on both cheeks Jannet thought cynically that he was an extremely handsome man. Just like a fairy prince, blond and shining and pure.

However, when he realised who stood so possessively beside Melly, the expression which tightened his features was far from regal. Confusion warred with fury; he swallowed hard twice before he regained enough control to wipe all traces of emotion from his face.

His arrival was unnoticed by Melly. Even as he set purposefully off towards her something Trent said surprised her into a crack of laughter. As his glowing head came a little closer to hers she looked up into his face, her own suddenly alight.

Derek hesitated, then moved on, one hand touching his tie in a little preening movement. When Melly saw him her vivacity died, there came a trace of guilt into her expression. Derek's eyes paused on her face, then swept on to meet his cousin's. The two men ignored Melly. His eyes never leaving the other man's face Derek touched Melly's arm in a proprietorial challenge while Trent looked at him with cool impassivity.

Then Derek made some comment and those around them laughed. Again he made that little preening gesture.

Jennet drank a mouthful of wine. She knew what that movement meant. Someone was going to feel the effects of Derek's fury before the night was out.

Aloud she asked remotely, 'Why didn't you tell Melly that I'd been in contact with Trent?'

'I didn't want her upset. Mistakenly, I thought that not even Brigit would be meddlesome enough to invite him,' Rafe told her, before asking silkily, 'did you put her up to it?'

'How could I?'

'Oh, I'm sure you're clever enough to manipulate her into it,' he said, giving her a blazing predatory smile which should have sent her shrieking from the room. His teeth showed white against the dark skin of his face and her skin heated into fire as she went under in a surge of pagan need, limitless, unrestrained.

Her ears rang with his low, fierce laughter. One arm encircled her, holding her pinned against his lean, hard strength. Jennet made a little bracing movement of her shoulders as if to carry a weight too heavy for them, and his arm tightened. Across the room Derek looked up and for a moment an expression of such dark malevolence distorted his face that Jennet flinched. Instantly it was gone, replaced by a smile which was almost normal. Oh God, Jennet thought, oh, what have I done?

Dinner seemed to drag on for hours. Lacking Te Puriri's enormous table and dining room Brigit had sensibly opted for a buffet, serving a meal which was surprisingly free from pretension. Jennet had no appetite, but Rafe insisted on filling her plate with delectable pieces of sesame chicken, some pasta salad and fresh asparagus. He refilled her wine glass as well as his own before bearing her off to sit on a small sofa in an almost secluded alcove.

Jennet eyed her plate with disfavour. Her stomach was churning, but she nibbled small portions, limiting herself to no more than half a glass of wine. Not so Derek, she noted with a chill. He appeared to be in tearing good spirits, talking a lot, eating practically nothing, and already as she watched he had disposed of four glasses of wine.

Beside him Melly was trying hard to hide her unease. Jennet knew exactly how she felt. Although more than anything else she wanted Derek off-balance, she could not help shrinking as she watched him, his gestures a little larger than life-size, eyes unnaturally bright in his flushed face.

Not too far away Trent Addison waited, his presence a safeguard for Melly in spite of the fact that just by being there he added fuel to Derek's rage.

'Time to go,' Brigit called, carefully averting her eyes from Rafe. 'We can't be too late!'

The Takapo Valley hall was large, a relic of the days after the Second World War when every community, however small, erected some sort of War Memorial. Hollingworth money had provided the wherewithal to build large and opulently; on a big kauri shield were engraved the names of all those who had died in that conflict. Two of the golden lines were Hollingworths, Dougal's older brother and a cousin.

But there was no sadness tonight. A committee had decorated the building with great bowls of spring flowers and greenery, the walls were lined with tables, nightclub style, and the entire district was determined to enjoy themselves and had dressed up in their most elegant clothes to just that purpose.

Even the band, brought up from Auckland, had allowed themselves to be persuaded to keep the music to a reasonable sound level.

The first dance was pre-empted by Rafe. Ignoring Jennet's protest he led her on to the floor, with a twisted smile, holding her so that she was pressed against him and slowly, inevitably, she responded to the insidious spell of his virility, stimulated almost beyond bearing by the play of his muscles as he moved, the effortless strength and grace, his potent aura of sexuality.

Holding herself rigidly she tried to pull away.

'What's the matter?' he asked in apparent innocence.

'I'm not in the market for dalliance,' she retorted, her lie achieving the colour of truth.

'I don't want to dally with you,' he said smoothly, tightening his arm so that she was brought up against him again. 'I want to take you. I want to own you so completely that when any subsequent lovers get you into bed it will be my face you see behind your eyelids, my name you call them by, my body you crave.'

Appalled, Jennet's lungs whistled as she dragged breath into them. Her head moved in swift negation but nothing could blunt the searing impact of his words. She did not need to look at him to comprehend his primitive elemental lust for the essence of her which even the restraints of civilisation could not control. He had shown her the hidden depths of his soul and she was terrified.

'No,' she said in a low voice.

'Oh yes. And you feel the same way. That's why it's

no use saying the multiplication table or quoting poetry to yourself to take your mind off me. You can't hide. The only poetry that comes to mind are love poems, and the sort of multiplication that I intend is strictly between two.'

Colour rioted through her skin and she groaned and turned her hot face into his shoulder.

He ended the small silence by muttering in a savage, goaded undertone, 'I want you, Jennet. I don't care what you are or what you're doing here. Why can't you accept that as your triumph and leave poor Derek alone?'

'Because I can't,' she said sadly, lifting her face to his. 'Rafe—I——'

As her voice faltered and then died away she saw his regard change, become transformed into contempt and scorn. It had held a quality close to tenderness; now he looked like a pirate, reckless and cruel, flaunting his vital charisma with no hint of mercy.

'Very well then,' he said between his teeth. 'You've made your bed. I hope you don't find the lying in it too painful.'

The music stopped then and he took her arm, threading his way through the dancers with less than his normal courtesy.

From then on the evening began to resemble those dreams marked by a series of scenes, isolated, unconnected, yet so vivid that when the sleeper wakes each one is like a picture in the brain. She danced with Rafe again, with most of the men in their party. Jennet knew that she laughed and talked, she must have made sense, but the moment the words left her mouth she couldn't remember what she had said.

Once she danced with Derek, suffered the alcohol smell on his breath and his greedy hold on her; she kept her eyes lowered so that she didn't have to face his glazed eyes.

They spoke little, but halfway through the dance he stopped moving, standing still in the middle of the floor oblivious to the startled stares from those around them while his eyes followed Melly's progress as she was whirled around in Trent's arms.

'Bastard,' he muttered, white beneath the alcohol flush.

Somebody called something to him and he realised where he was and swore and took Jennet back into his arms. But when the music stopped he left her, plunging through the dancers with complete disregard for them.

At some stage Trent solicited the next dance. Flashing him a meaningless smile she rose and went into his arms while a little distance away Derek finished yet more wine and set his glass down with a small crash on the table.

'Enjoying yourself?' Trent murmured. He had a deep, rather gravelly voice.

'Not in the least.'

'Then allow me to congratulate you on your excellent acting.'

'Oh Lord,' she groaned, 'I wish tonight was over. Trent, I'm so frightened.'

Like most strong men he was intensely protective. 'Listen,' he said urgently, 'You must not let him catch you alone. I'll be watching——'

'*No!* You stay well out of it.'

'I don't like it.'

'Neither do I,' she shivered, 'but there's no other way. Do you think I haven't tried? He's guarded his back too well. Thank God he's drinking. He was—well, alcohol always loosened any inhibitions he might have had.'

'You'd think with all that he has at stake, he'd have kept on the wagon tonight.'

With sombre intensity she said, 'He doesn't think he has anything to worry about. He's convinced Rafe, you see, and he must know that I haven't told Melly about—about the violence. He thinks he's home and dry. The only thing that is worrying him is your presence, and that is what is going to push him over the edge.'

His hand clenched on hers, making her wince. 'Sorry,' he said abruptly. 'Correct me if I'm wrong, but it seems to me that you are trying to tell me that you expect him to—attack Melissa.'

'Yes.'

'No,' he said softly. 'I won't allow it.'

'It has to be that way,' she hesitated, then went on urgently, 'he's already angry with her. Look at them now; they're quarrelling. Melly is not a meek, milk and water miss, she won't back off if he wants a fight.'

'No,' he repeated harshly.

'Trent, I'll try to deflect him but—at least promise me that you won't interfere.'

'No.'

She bit her lip. 'Then you run the risk of ruining everything. I honestly believe that even if he hits me she'll think I deserve it.'

He gritted out an imprecation, then said with such reluctance that she didn't quite trust him, 'Very well, but I don't want her hurt.'

'That's what this is all about,' she said wearily. 'Remember?'

His eyes softened. 'Yes, of course I do. I'm sorry. This must be absolute hell for you.'

She looked very seriously into his raffish, striking face, saw there a desperation which told her far more than his words. 'No,' she said carefully, 'it's not too bad. He can no longer hurt me——'

'If he marries Melissa, won't that hurt?'

Her shoulders lifted. 'That's why we must provoke him beyond bearing tonight. There'll be no other chance.'

'Then why won't you let me——'

It was her turn to interrupt. 'I don't want him dead,' she said tonelessly.

He was silent for some minutes after that before he said in quite a different voice, 'What will you do if this doesn't come off?'

'Tell Rafe, impress it on him. He won't believe me but he'll keep an eye on them.' She smiled wryly. 'Like all strong men he's very protective and he and Melly love each other. She'll go to him.'

'What is it between you two?'

'You have obviously noticed that Rafe and I do not get on.'

There was a note of cynical amusement in his voice as he said. 'Then why does he watch you as if you are his only chance of salvation? I've seen him with quite a few women, at least one of whom he was having an affair with, and he's never wasted that kind of emotion on any of them.'

'Pull the other one,' she said pleasantly.

He grinned, but obeyed her unspoken command and dropped the subject.

And then it was the last dance and Rafe swept her on to the floor. He held her loosely but she could sense the leashed anger vibrating through his lean, elegant body. The aura of danger which had kept her alert all evening suddenly hovered ominously over her, like some elemental act of nature.

Not once did he speak. Occasionally she lifted her eyes to let them linger on the rigid line of his jaw; his eyes were narrowed slivers of jet. Beneath her hand taut muscles spoke of tension and control. And something else. He was, she thought warily, on an adrenalin high, prepared for danger, wary yet confident as a beast of prey threatened in its own jungle.

Somehow Melly came home with them. The atmosphere in the car was brittle and crackling but all three remained in control. About fifty people arrived at Te Puriri, determined to keep the party going. Although exhausted Jennet slipped into her role as co-hostess with Melly, unobtrusively watching Derek who had arrived with a noisy group of people and who was still drinking, albeit more slowly. She knew the signs, only too well. He was in a white rage, fuelled by alcohol and Melly's aloofness and Trent Addison's presence. Always such a fury had escalated into violence.

Rafe, too, was watching him. He was too astute not to recognise that something ugly was brewing in spite of Derek's ready smile and boisterous high spirits. Once Rafe's eyes met Jennet's; she thought that there was a gleam of comprehension in their cold brilliance, but as he turned away immediately she couldn't be sure.

Here, amongst his neighbours, he was an urbane host, upholding the station's traditions of hospitality. This was not one of the grand occasions when Te Puriri's guests flew in by plane or came in opulent cars and displayed the sort of jewellery which normally saw only the interior of safes and bank vaults, but it was when Te Puriri revealed its true self, a working station in a farming district. And Rafe stood out head and shoulders, the big man of the district, as he would be anywhere.

The party had by now entered a noisy phase when only singing, it seemed, would satisfy many of the guests. A shy woman, a newcomer to the district, was coaxed towards the piano. Blushing, smiling, she looked rather helplessly towards Rafe.

'I can't,' she protested. 'It's a beautiful instrument.'

He gave her a smile which visibly stopped her in her tracks. 'It's tough,' he told her, 'And I know that you are a musician. Don't worry, no one will park their glasses on it.'

'They'd better not,' she returned, emboldened, as she sat down before it.

Rafe was right. She was an excellent musician. On some less boisterous occasion Jennet would have liked to hear her play up to her level, but tonight she was asked for *Tavern in the Town*, and from there swung into other songs, both old and modern, all eminently singable.

Draining the mineral water which was all that she had been drinking for some hours now, Jennet's eyes traversed the huge room which had once been a warren of pantries and sculleries and laundries. Diana had seen the potential and had them transformed into this huge room, perfect for this kind of informal entertaining. On more formal occasions the drawing-room and the ballroom were used.

Everyone—almost everyone, she corrected—appeared to be enjoying themselves. Those who didn't want to sing were clustered at the other end of the room, talking. A high pitched laugh drew Jennet's eyes to a woman in a blue skin-tight dress who was flirting rather desperately with Trent, clearly fascinated by his saturnine smile. No one had obviously drunk too much. Not even Derek ... slowly, as inconspicuously as possible, her gaze searched the room. No sign of Derek. Or Melly. Unconsciously her teeth worried her lower lip. Rafe was talking to an elderly couple, his charm never more apparent.

Where was Melly? She couldn't have been gone long, otherwise Trent would have been gone too. Jennet didn't trust him to keep the promise she had extracted from him, not if he thought Melly was being hurt.

Moving with a little less than her usual grace, willing herself to be inconspicuous, Jennet made her way to the door. Outside in the hall the muffled noise from the singers, now cheerfully rendering the *59th Street Bridge Song*, prevented her ears from picking up any other sounds. Moving down the hall she shook her head, trying to clear her hearing.

Suddenly her head swivelled. Had that been a small, choked noise coming from—where? Silence, during which she held her breath. Yes, a kind of moan followed by a man's voice. Derek's voice, and it came from the boudoir. Treading softly as a cat Jennet headed for the closed door. There was no further sound. Nervously her fingers twisted the handle.

Even though she knew what was happening behind that door the reality made her drag in a sharp painful breath. Melly was hunched over, her mouth open, eyes glazed in the intense self-absorption that only pain brings. Her hands were clasped together below her breast and little, choking noises were forced through her lips as she gasped for breath.

Derek had hit her in the solar plexus. He was standing with his back to Jennet, his hands cupped at his sides. As Jennet began to move he grabbed Melly's black hair, dragging her head up to meet his. Her face was contorted with terror and pain.

'You little bitch,' he said lightly, almost pleasantly, and slapped her face.

Melly made a pitiful attempt to ward off the blows but he laughed and jerked her wrists away.

'Leave her alone,' Jennet ordered thinly.

He froze. Then, slowly, he dropped Melly's hands and turned, his face blazing in cruel exultation.

'Well, well, well,' he said, smiling, as he came towards her, stalking her.

He looked like a demon, almost beside himself with the rage she remembered so well. Yet there was a dreadful restraint about him, and she remembered that, too.

He was not expecting resistance. Why should he? Like Melly, Jennet had only ever tried to protect herself from his hands and those attempts, feeble though they were, had always maddened him into further violence.

So he walked confidently towards her, still smiling, even handsome if you didn't look behind the false persona he had manufactured so skilfully. Only his eyes gave him away, glittering unnaturally, and his hands, balled into fists.

Jennet waited. At exactly the right moment she kicked, aiming at his most vulnerable part. He saw her intention and twisted sideways so that her foot missed its target. His hand lunged for her ankle but she was too quick and stepped back, rocking on her heels. He kept coming and she blocked his swinging fists and brought her knee up. An obscene grunt tore at his throat; his hands covered himself and he began to collapse on to his knees, eyes glazed.

Melly burst into a torrent of tears and flung herself into Rafe's arms as he came in through the door like a dark avenging angel. Above the tangle of Melly's hair Jennet, pale now, and trembling, met the bitter anger in his eyes as she rubbed the forearm Derek had hit.

'Hush, love,' he said soothingly, pulling Melly into his arms. 'It's all right, it's all over . . .'

'Oh, God,' Melly sobbed into his shoulder. 'He—he hit me . . . he said . . . he said I was flirting . . .'

'It's over,' Rafe repeated, his voice revealing none of the savage anger which was stark in his forbidding expression, 'Don't cry, Melly, it's finished.'

On the floor Derek made a retching noise. Jennet's eyes were fixed on Rafe's long fingers as they moved rhythmically across Melly's back, but she thought light-headedly that the lessons in self-defence had paid off. Then the blood drummed deafeningly in her ears. She swayed, put out a hand to steady herself on the back of a chair and bit her lip. Her eyes cleared and she straightened. Avoiding even looking at Derek she moved across to where Melly still wept in Rafe's strong arms.

'Come on, Mel,' she said quietly, her voice flat and emptied of feeling. 'I'll take you up to your room.'

With a shaking hand, Rafe smoothed the tumbled curls back from Melly's forehead. As he put Melly away from him he looked into her wet, stricken face with such bleak savagery that Jennet shuddered.

When she came down the stairs reaction had set in, and she was cold and aching. She hesitated for a moment outside the boudoir door, looking along the hall to where sounds of singing denoted that the party was still going strong.

As she watched the door opened and Trent came out, his expression aggressive.

'No,' she mouthed, shaking her head, but although he checked when he saw her, he didn't stop. Quickly she went to meet him.

'What the hell's happening?' he demanded.

'It's over,' she said with swift certainty.

'Melissa?'

'She's asleep,' she answered his unspoken question. 'She's all right, Trent. Upset, but not shattered. I don't think she was in love with him, really.'

'Of course she wasn't. She's in love with me.'

Jennet smiled a little wistfully at his unconscious arrogance. 'Well, if she is, she'll be fine. Hasn't Rafe come back yet?'

'No.'

'Oh. Well, can you sort of act as—as host? I know it's an imposition, but—we should be back soon.'

He hesitated, then gave her a wry, self-mocking smile. 'O.K., I'll subdue my instincts.'

Jennet sighed as she turned back to the room where she had left the two men; she hoped that Trent would get his desire.

Inside the boudoir, Derek was sitting on the sofa, his head in his hands, breathing stertorously. Rafe lounged against the wall with his hands in his pockets. Those wide shoulders were slightly slumped and the spare, chiselled lines of his face hid any emotions.

Both men looked across as Jennet came in but it was Derek who spoke first.

'I should have finished you off when I had the chance,' he said thickly; the words were barely distinguishable and his face was distorted, manic.

Rafe's voice cracked across his like a whip. 'That will do,' he commanded, and when Derek subsided into silence he asked, 'How is she?'

'I just gave her a sleeping pill. It worked very quickly.'

'Was that wise?'

She nodded. 'It was a mild one, and she drank very little during the evening. I was watching her. It won't harm her.'

It hurt to look at him. She had wanted to be vindicated in his eyes, but not at such cost. A less controlled man might have shown his feelings, but Rafe's head was like a bronze bust, the cold perfection of his features successfully hiding all emotions but an incredible tension. Even his eyes were hooded, the long long lashes casting curling shadows beneath them.

'So,' the deep voice said tonelessly, 'what do we do now?'

Derek blustered, 'You have no right——'

'Shut up,' Rafe said. He could have been reading a list, but something in the even, dispassionate voice stopped the other man's protest without a second's hesitation.

'Will she testify against him?' The black eyes met hers above Derek's head.

What did he want? Derek shot to his feet, hands clenching ominously at his sides as he turned to face Rafe. Once Jennet would have trembled at this, distraught with terror. Now she watched without emotion, and thought serenely, I'm free, and wondered why she wasn't lyrical with joy.

'You can't do that,' Derek threatened, flushed now,

his head thrust pugnaciously forward. 'Who the hell do you think you are, you bloody—just because you're the high and mighty Hollingworths you think you can do anything. Well, just try it! She won't testify against me.' He swung back to stare at Jennet. 'You never did, did you, Jennet? A woman can't——'

'But Melly is not your wife,' Rafe pointed out with insulting indifference. 'What did you do to her?'

Jennet told him. Again Rafe ignored Derek's protest, his deep voice clear and flat in the sullen silence.

'Well, will she testify?'

Again that commanding stare. Slowly, feeling her way, Jennet said, 'Yes of course she will, Rafe, if you want her to. There's no way she'll marry him now.'

'Christ,' Derek said, the soft word slurring through lips which were suddenly slack as he lunged towards her. 'I'll kill you, you bitch, I'll——'

'Lay one finger on her and I'll take you apart.' Rafe's voice was so heavy with menace that the hairs on the back of Jennet's neck stood up straight.

It stopped Derek. He turned from Jennet to the man who watched them both, baring his teeth. 'Yes, you want her,' he said viciously. 'You've always wanted her, haven't you? You won't get any joy out of her, you fool. She's all come-hither, she turns your guts to water with wanting her but it's like taking an icicle to bed.'

There was a moment of quiet, humming with danger. Rafe didn't move, not a muscle, not an eyelash, yet Jennet felt a wave of emotion emanating from him.

'If you beat the hell out of her, it's no wonder,' he retorted offensively. 'I don't have the same trouble.'

Jennet's breath stopped in her throat. With dilated eyes she watched as Derek's body tensed but he too was aware of the danger Rafe represented.

'She's a cold bitch,' he said unevenly. 'A tease. My God, you've seen her in action, man. She's spent her time playing us off against each other. I'll——'

'You'll do nothing.' The words crackled across the silent room. 'Jennet is no longer your wife. And you'll not get your hands on Melly, either.'

The smooth, pale head shook from side to side as if Derek was trying to clear his thoughts.

Remorselessly Rafe continued. 'It's over. You've lost everything. After the court case you'll be branded as a wife-beater, you'll be less than nothing. People despise bullies. There'll be no chance of you marrying again without someone filling any prospective wife in on the details of your—aberration.'

Derek swayed back on his heels, his face livid. One hand tightened into a fist, but when he looked at the frightening dark figure that was Rafe, the fingers straightened again. He cursed under his breath.

Without mercy Rafe's deep voice resumed, 'Your friends will avoid you, you won't be able to show your face at any parties. No more ski trips, no more . . .'

'Rafe, no!' Jennet didn't know why she objected. With implacable accuracy Rafe had chosen to attack in a manner guaranteed to drive Derek beyond reason.

Now he made a thick noise in his throat, glaring at Rafe with murder in his eyes. He looked like a maddened bull the moment before it closes its eyes and charges.

'You won't be welcome anywhere,' Rafe taunted and at last moved, turning his back on them in a gesture as deliberate as it was insulting.

So it was only Jennet who saw the fury in Derek's expression transmute into something else, an emotion she didn't recognise. For a moment he hesitated, staring at the broad shoulders and athlete's body of the man who had so accurately pointed out his future, and then he turned his head so that he was looking at Jennet.

'If you'd loved me . . .' he said incredibly, his tone almost pleading. 'I wanted you to love me. You drove me mad . . .'

Jennet closed her eyes in pain, recognising that he spoke what he thought was the truth.

Her tacit rejection was met with a harsh indrawn breath before he swung to face Rafe once more. 'As for you,' he said with gloating emphasis, 'you'll rot in the kind of hell she put me in. And I'll laugh ... I'll laugh ...'

A moment later he was gone.

'Where are you going?'

Rafe's voice hurt. Jennet stopped in her headlong rush towards the door.

'We can't let him go like that,' she begged, her glance agonised. 'He was beside himself. Rafe?'

As he moved with swift litheness towards her she flinched away from the anger in him, afraid of him as she had never been of Derek's violence.

'Oh, *don't*!' he jerked out, trying to speak calmly. His hands enveloping her shaking ones, the thumbs rubbing over the fine skin, his mouth twisting in torment. 'I wanted him to try to take me,' he admitted harshly. 'It's just as well he's a coward. I'd have killed him and enjoyed doing it.'

The self-contempt in his voice, and that deadly, cold anger, made Jennet wince. Each stark word hit her like a blow.

'No,' she whispered, trying vainly to pull her hands free so that she could cover her face, that collection of features which had been the cause of all this. Derek's appeal had burnt into her brain.

'I wish I'd never been born. So much violence ...' Guilt closed her throat.

'What the hell are you talking about?' When she couldn't reply, wouldn't meet his eyes, he insisted, 'Answer me, Jennet. You stupid little fool, how can you blame yourself?'

'You heard him,' she said quietly, staring with empty eyes at their linked hands as he pressed hers against the hard wall of his chest. Beneath the silk of his shirt she felt the heavy beat of his life force.

'I didn't love him,' she explained hopelessly. 'I never did. When—after we were married, I couldn't—he ...' The words dried on her tongue. How could she explain to Rafe what she had only just realised herself, that her heart had been his since she was sixteen!

'Come and sit down,' he said, sliding his arm around her waist to urge her across to the sofa. 'Poor Jennet, you're shaking. I'll go and get you some brandy.'

'No,' she said, but he returned with a half a glass of it, the savage anger subsiding as he gentled her, coaxing her to drink it.

'We should go back,' she protested.

He gave her an extremely sardonic smile, the frightening stranger gone, once more the Rafe she knew so well. 'We're not being missed. Everyone's having a marvellous time singing ribald songs from their university days, with Addison in charge.'

'Oh,' she said faintly and sipped the brandy, welcoming its biting strength.

When it was half gone he said, 'Thank you for coming back, Jennet.'

Waves of tiredness submerged her, floated away with the inhibitions which had kept her silent for so many years. 'It—I felt I had to,' she said slowly. 'I went to a psychiatrist when I got Diana's letter telling me they were engaged. He said that Derek would probably beat Melly as he did me and I couldn't bear that thought. I didn't want to come back but I had to.'

'How did it start?'

'Right at the beginning.' She sighed, lashes dropping, her mouth very vulnerable. 'You know, every magazine tells you that with all the sport girls play, the first time you make love is a breeze. It is, too, for most girls. It didn't happen that way with me. I fainted. Afterwards I realised that that was the first sign. He seemed—elated, in a queer sort of way. I thought it was because it proved that I was a virgin. How could I know?'

'How could you indeed?' His voice was very gentle, not like Rafe at all. 'Finish the rest of your drink.'

Obediently she swallowed it down, accepting, even welcoming the fact that it made her head swim. She was floating, disassociated from that quiet voice and the man whose arm held her against his shoulder.

'After that it was hell,' she said remotely, closing her eyes against the hand which stroked the nape of her neck. 'By the time we got back from the honeymoon I dreaded making love. And he liked that, too.'

Rafe muttered something ugly under his breath and shifted, taking the glass from her. His other hand covered her twisting writhing ones in her lap. He had discarded his coat; beneath the silk shirt he was very hard and warm.

Sighing, Jennet said, 'I know now that he's been conditioned to see violence as a solution, but at the time all I knew was that I was terrified of him and I was—alone. I didn't know what to do. I did realise that in some strange frightening way it excited him to hurt me.'

It was impossible to open her eyes; they were heavy, stuck together. Her skin prickled as she recalled the dread Derek had roused in her.

'Go on,' Rafe prompted evenly.

'The first time he actually beat me was after a party. He'd had a few drinks although he wasn't drunk. He said I'd spent the evening flirting with someone. I tried to defend myself but it was useless, he just got angrier. So after that I only talked to the women. You must remember—you were at several of those parties that year.'

In spite of herself, her voice shook. Rafe's arm tightened. That the comfort was impersonal didn't upset her. He had misjudged her and now he was showing his remorse and the combination of brandy and adrenalin in her bloodstream was making it impossible for her to resist such a dangerous situation. Tomorrow things would be back to normal; not even tonight's traumatic events could expunge the fact that she was Diana's daughter and so suspect forever in Rafe's eyes. But for just this once she was going to rely shamelessly on his great strength to see her through.

'I remember,' he said without expression. 'Oh, yes, I remember very clearly.'

'So then he said that I made him look a fool because I didn't mix. In the end he didn't really need an excuse.' She dragged the breath into her lungs. 'You know, looking back I think I must have been insane with fear. I didn't know what to do. Diana was overseas—but I don't know that I would have told her even if she'd been here. It's incredible but he even managed to convince me that it was my fault. I didn't love him and he told me that he loved me, that I drove him mad because I was so cold.'

'Why on earth didn't you come to me? You must have known that I'd have helped.'

The harsh question made her flinch. Half beneath her breath she said, 'You—that was the year you were abroad so much. I think it was America you went to.'

'Don't try to condone my behaviour,' he said bleakly. 'I know why you didn't feel that you could expect any help from me. I was a blind, prejudiced fool. I should have noticed that something was wrong.'

'It wasn't your fault,' she whispered. 'I couldn't bring myself to tell *anyone*, Rafe.'

'But if I hadn't been so bloody censorious and arrogant . . . So *blind*, so wilfully, deliberately blind . . .'

'No, no!' She stared up into his face, dark now with torment and self-contempt. She couldn't bear that he should be wracked by such anguish. 'Rafe, don't! He was so clever. He made sure that there weren't any of the sort of bruises which might give him away. And if you remember, he was always charming to me in company; he used that charm like a weapon.'

'Oh, I remember,' he said grimly, his fingers clenching on hers until they hurt. 'I used to watch you ...' He broke off abruptly.

Cuddled in against his shoulder, Jennet could hear and feel his breathing, taste the scent of him, masculine and exciting. The tender, sensuous stroke of his thumb across her palm was an erotic little caress which made her acutely conscious that she had to free herself before she was betrayed by her reactions.

'Rafe, we'll have to go back to the party,' she said huskily, forcing herself to straighten up. He let her go and she stood, one hand on his shoulder to support her rubbery legs.

He stayed sitting, his expression sombre, then looked up at her and smiled with bitter irony. 'You're right, of course. Hospitality is a sacred duty.'

If it was, he rather abused it. Within fifteen minutes everyone had left, most of them convinced that the decision had been theirs alone.

Even Trent had gone although the long, considering look he gave Jennet indicated that very soon she was going to have to tell him exactly what had happened.

CHAPTER TEN

RAFE and Jennet turned away from the door just as the telephone shrilled its urgent summons. Jennet felt a faint premonition of doom as Rafe picked up the receiver.

'Yes?' he said shortly. Then his expression changed into that hardness he wore to cloak emotion. His eyes fixed on to Jennet, slim and exhausted in her black dress in the dimness of the doorway. 'Where? Are you *sure*? How—oh yes, I see. All right, I'll be right down.'

'Rafe, what is it?'

He replaced the receiver heavily. 'That was Trevor Brown. He has the dairy farm by the Takapo stream. He heard a car go over the bridge. It was Derek.'

'And . . .?' She didn't dare articulate the words, as if saying them might give them substance, make them into solid realities.

'He's dead.'

She gasped, her hands flying to her breast.

'I goaded him into it,' he said harshly.

'No, Rafe.'

'You heard me. You stood there and heard me taunt him. I did it coldly and deliberately.' The cold mask hid his emotions, but she could feel the pain in him. 'I wanted to hurt him as you had been hurt. Instead I pushed him over the edge.'

Jennet ran across to where he stood. Her hands reached up, enclosing his lean face, the fingers curving around the high, stark cheekbones. Her voice was urgent yet very tender, compelling belief. 'Rafe, you didn't want him dead, did you?'

He focused on her face with difficulty. 'Didn't I?'

She stood on tiptoes, willing him to respond, to convince him in spite of the resistance she felt in his rigid body. 'Even if you did, darling, he has always been a bad driver, careless, pushing his luck, While we were married he had two accidents, I'll bet there have been several others since then.'

Slowly he nodded, his gaze lingering on the sweet curve of her mouth, the earnest conviction in her beautiful face.

'I'm sorry,' she said. 'Sorry that he's dead, but, Rafe, he would never have got help, would he? He was too arrogant. Sooner or later there would have been another woman like Melly and me.' Her hands slid down his neck, touched the dark hair at the nape before she hugged him fiercely to her. 'That psychiatrist I went to said that violence is self-perpetuating. Derek had probably been beaten as a child, or seen his father beat his mother. If he had children they would have grown up like him.'

'All that doesn't alter the fact that I sent him over that bridge,' he said raggedly.

Jennet took heart from the fact that he didn't push her away. 'Darling, it wasn't just you. He'd been drinking heavily then he was forced to face up to what he was and accept the fact that he'd lost Melly.'

His eyes swept her face as his hands moved slowly to hold her pressed against him in a fierce embrace without passion.

Slowly his head bent; into her hair he said quietly, 'Thank you, Jennet. You are—very kind. Don't wait up for me.'

He meant it, so, after stacking the glasses into the dishwasher, she went upstairs, her feet dragging slightly. She felt strange, unreal, a sensation which persisted while she undressed and went to see how Melly was. Resting quietly, Melly's face was smoothed by a deep, dreamless sleep. As she stood for a moment watching

her Jennet remembered Trent Addison's expression
when she had whispered that the engagement was off.
He hadn't smiled, but the clever, cynical face had
relaxed. Whatever he felt for this half-sister of hers, it
wasn't just the cold desire to seduce. Only time would
tell, of course, but perhaps Melly could find happiness
with him.

Quietly Jennet set off towards her bedroom. At her
doorway she hesitated, frowning. It was a cold night,
getting colder, and when Rafe got back he would be
freezing. She decided to put his electric blanket on.

Since he had become the owner of Te Puriri she had
never set foot in the suite of rooms set aside for him.
The bedroom was austere now, a far cry from the
mannered opulence of Diana's reign. Someone very
talented had decorated it in muted browns and blacks
relieved only by touches of gold. A highly dramatic
room, she decided, looping the belt of her dressing-
gown around one hand as she pivoted slowly, her eyes
taking in the huge bed, a wall of books, a splendid
modern chest of drawers, Italian by the smooth
sophistication of line and proportion, and an antique
secretaire which was equally sophisticated and just as
superbly proportioned.

In this room, in that bed, a woman's white skin
would have all the sheen and allure of a pearl.

'I love you,' she whispered to its absent owner, her
hand switching the electric blanket on then covering her
mouth as she yawned. The bed was immensely inviting
but some sense of self-preservation steered her to one of
the armchairs by the French windows. Yawning again,
she collapsed into it. Just for a second, she promised
herself, she would stay just for a few moments until she
summoned the strength to get back to her own bed.

Twice she caught herself nodding and jerked awake,
but the third time her pale head slid sideways across the
back of the chair and she slept.

The dream began slowly, as if she had woken up from a deep sleep. Her first sensation was of warmth and the smoothness of sheets against her skin and a feeling of well-being so profound that she smiled in the darkness and made a funny little noise in her throat, half grunt, half yawn.

She was in bed but she was not alone. Nothing touched her but she could feel the heat of a man's body, feel his presence.

In the way of dreams she knew that it was Rafe who lay breathing peacefully beside her. Freed from the constraints of reality she whispered his name into the darkness and was not surprised when he turned from his back to his side so that he lay facing her. She said his name again and put out her hand and touched his face, knowing by instinct where it would be. Against her fingers his skin was warm and slightly rough as she followed the hard line of his jaw. He said nothing but his hand came up to her shoulder, smoothing the skin, caressing the outline of her shoulder-blade and spine, all heaven in his touch. She sucked in her breath and her fingers trembled against the firm shape of his mouth. Slowly his hand found its way down the sensitive inner skin of her arm until his hand reached hers, holding it still against his lips.

He rubbed his jaw against the palm, a tiny abrasive movement which set her nerves tingling with delight. Then his warm mouth moved from finger to finger, kissing, biting gently, suckling, until her breath came swiftly past her throat and the steady beat of her heart began to pick up speed.

Yet except for his hand over hers and his mouth against it they were not touching. Only in a dream could such a small contact be the most tantalising caress that she had ever experienced.

From a centre deep within, heat began to build, a slow strange combustion that spread by degrees throughout her entire body, kindling fires in pleasure points of whose existence she had never known until now.

When his mouth left her hand she whimpered softly with disappointment, but he said unevenly, 'Touch me, darling,' and guided her fingers to the place where his neck met the bare width of his shoulder.

Only in a dream could she permit herself to respond so wantonly, only in a dream could she know that to skim her hand over the expanse of smooth supple skin was to give him exquisite pleasure, almost as much as it gave her to touch him. Her hand drifted lower, tracking pathways through the tangle of hair across his chest, explored the strong cage of his ribs, spread over the exact spot where his heart slammed into her palm.

The wall of his chest lifted, then fell as if breathing had become painful to him. Drawn by his strength and her need she moved closer to him, but still they were not touching, only her head was close enough for her lips to meet his throat. She pressed a kiss there, and wondered how it would feel to explore him with her mouth.

His skin was taut, slightly damp yet hot. Tentatively Jennet touched it with her tongue, enjoyed the masculine taste and touched it again while her hand slid down his ribs towards his hip.

'Do you know what you're doing?'

The question made her laugh. This was a dream, who knew what was going to happen in a dream?

Her lips moved against the skin of his throat as she told him. Her wide-open hand came to rest across his flat stomach. Beneath it the strong muscles tensed.

'Jennet,' he said in a strange, thickened voice.

'Hush,' she whispered, kissing up his throat and beneath his chin. 'I love you. This is all I'll have. Don't spoil my dream.'

He lowered his head, caught her mouth with his and

kissed the tremulous width of it, tiny soft kisses which stirred her unbearably so that she moaned into his mouth.

Then he said, 'Very well, I won't spoil your dream. I love you.'

Of course he did. That was what dreams were for. To give you the momentary illusion of happiness.

'Then kiss me properly,' she begged.

So he did and it was joy and ecstasy for this time there was no anger, no contempt, no driving need to conquer. His kiss was sweet. He coaxed her lips apart to taste the soft depths revealed to him yet she was not frightened or repelled, not even when he slid an arm across her back and pulled her close to him, and she realised that, like her, he was naked, and, like her, he was very, very aroused.

'You are so beautiful,' she whispered.

He laughed, a deep soft sound in his throat. 'Men aren't beautiful. You are the beautiful one, so beautiful I ache when I see you and my bones shake in my body with wanting you.'

Then he took the initiative, his mouth assessing the contours of her face, pushing her head back so that her throat was a bow for his kisses. She shivered as his teeth bit gently down the arc of it and without knowing what she did, her body twisted fiercely against him. In this dark bed, in this dark room, she knew exactly what she wanted, had wanted for years, and because it was a dream she could ask him openly.

'I want you to love me,' she whispered.

'I do,' he vowed, his breath searing across her sensitised skin. 'I will. It's going to be like no other time for us both.'

His words made her body leap into life, excited her to boldness. Smiling into the darkness she said, 'And you will never forget. Whenever you dream, you'll wish that I was with you, like this.'

'I have, for years,' he said on a groan. His hand slid across her skin to cup her breast.

Needles of sharp desire transfixed her with pleasure so acute that it was almost pain. Gasping, she twisted on to her back, her hands clenching on to his skin.

'Rafe,' she cried, shattering as her body writhed into abandon, 'Rafe, I can't—I want——'

'I feel like the lord of all things,' he muttered. 'As if this world and everything in it is mine because you are my world and from now on you belong to me.'

His mouth fastened on to her breast, closed over the erect nub, warm and moist and fantastically exciting. The gentle tugging made Jennet groan in anticipation and frustration, her body in flames, as her hands pulled at the smooth hardness of his shoulders, urging him silently to take her with the strength and power she had craved for so long.

'Please,' she pleaded, barely able to form the word because she was shivering with fever, forlorn, empty, racked by desire.

'Yes, now!' he said triumphantly.

Then at last she felt the weight of his body and knew the fierce rapture of his possession. She was overwhelmed by sensation yet it was fulfilment, soaring ecstasy which tore his name from her lips in an agony of supplication until her body convulsed beneath and about him and she went sobbing over the edge into darkness, his muffled groan echoing in her ears as his body trembled in ecstasy.

For of course it wasn't a dream. And she had known, right from the moment she woke. This was Rafe's bed, in Rafe's bedroom. She had just seduced him and it had been like a foretaste of heaven. And now would come the reckoning.

She lay with her breath catching in her throat, eyes tightly closed against him, weighed down by his still shuddering body while her brain screamed at her to run, anywhere, away from this shame above all others. But she couldn't move. His heart was beating so loudly that she could only just hear the heavy rasp of his breathing. When at last the frantic hammering of his heart began to slow to something like normality she tried to move away.

'No.' His voice was barely audible as though he was having difficulty speaking, but the hand that pinned her to the pillows was uncompromising.

'No,' he said again, more strongly. 'You're not going to leave me, not now, not ever again. I won't let you. This is real, Jennet, my heart's love, my dearest girl. I've waited so long for you. You've always belonged to me only I was too stubborn to accept it. Can you forgive me for that?'

Dumbfounded, she could not answer.

After a silent moment he moved, lifting himself on to the mattress beside her. She flinched as his arms crushed her against the hard length of his body, holding her in a grip as strong as death, as strong as love.

'Do you want me to beg?' he muttered into her hair. 'I'll do that. I'll do anything I must to keep you here. Only tell me again that you love me, tell me that you'll never leave me.'

She could not bear it. Tears burned beneath her eyelids and she choked.

Very quietly he soothed, 'It's all over, darling. It's all right. You're safe now.'

Sobs tore through her, heavy and cleansing, washing away the brittle crust the years had formed over her emotions. Rafe was wonderfully gentle, holding her tenderly until she was gasping and empty, snuffling miserably into the handkerchief he found for her.

'Oh, hell,' she muttered drearily.

His chest lifted in a soundless chuckle. 'Feel better?'

'I feel as though I've been through the wringer.' She stretched and gave a small squeak of shock, calling on flippancy to cover the profound emotional turmoil which his shattering disclosure had produced. 'All of me, you brute. What did you do to me? You don't know your own strength!'

'Not used to the exercise, darling?' When she flinched he muttered something beneath his breath and scooped her against him, his mouth on her forehead. 'Have there been any other men for you since you ran away from Derek?'

'No,' she said simply. 'I thought I was frigid. That's why——'

She was stopped by an enormous yawn and the conviction that she was talking too much.

But he prompted, with a hint of the implacable determination she knew well, 'That's why what?'

She capitulated. 'Why I was so shocked when I came back and you—and I—well, if you must know, I took one look at you and I was sixteen again and in all the turmoil of an adolescent crush. Every time I looked at you or you looked at me I went hot and cold and prickly. It was just as though the years between had never happened. I was furious and frightened and excited.'

'And now?'

'Oh, now.' A few hours ago she would almost have gone to her death rather than have him know this. 'Now,' she said sweetly, 'I love you.'

'After only three days?'

'I always have, since before I knew what it was all about. It's just deepened over the years.'

Very quietly he said, 'I don't mind if it's only desire as yet, Jennet. God knows I've done nothing to make you love me, I've behaved like a swine to you for years. And it's no excuse that everything I've said and done was because I loved you and despised myself for it. You want me, that's enough to build on. I'll do everything I can to persuade you into loving me but I want the truth now. There must be no lies between us, not ever again.'

So he still didn't trust her, or himself. It would take years for her to prove that she loved him, but she would do it. She was strong enough for anything!

She hugged him to her, moving so that she cradled the dark weight of his head against her breast, holding his strength to the softness of her body.

'Oh, I love you,' she said, resting her cheek on the crisp hair, her tone making the statement into a vow. 'I want you, make no mistake about that, but I'd love you if you never touched me again. It's lasted for more years than I care to remember, most of them spent away from you. I might stop loving you when I die, but I doubt it.'

'Darling,' he said thickly. 'Oh, my darling, I know. I'm incomplete without you, half a man.'

'Yes.'

How long they lay entwined in an embrace without passion Jennet didn't know. Perhaps they slept. If they did it was to wake in the same position.

She asked quietly, 'Why didn't you kick me out, Rafe?'

'I wanted to know why you'd felt forced to come back. I knew it wasn't just mischief.' He reacted to her astonishment with a smile, turned it into a kiss before saying, 'Oh, I had you tarred with Diana's brush, but although I refused to admit it, I've always known that you weren't that sort. To be completely frank, neither is Diana. She's totally self-centred, completely selfish, just as amoral as a cat and with a cat's blithe disregard for anything but her own comfort, but she had the virtues of her vices as well, and she didn't ever make mischief just for the fun of it. There was always a reason. And although she's malicious, she's never been vindictive. Neither have you.'

Shaken by his cruelly dispassionate judgment she

tightened her arms around him, leaning her cheek on to his head. The stringy thickness of his hair was a pleasant friction against her skin, the clean, tantalising masculine scent of him stimulated her. Dreamily she forced herself to listen to the deep beautiful voice.

'When I caught you off-guard, you looked haunted. And although you hid it well, I sensed your fear of Derek and it made me wonder. You've never been afraid of me, and God knows, I've given you enough cause.' He paused before finishing, 'And I was never entirely happy with Melly's engagement to him. There was nothing I could put my finger on, but something didn't ring true.'

'Poor Derek,' she sighed. 'To die so young.'

'Yes.'

They were silent, each thinking of him, then abruptly Rafe said, 'All the same, he could have done something about it. He must have known that there was help available for him if he asked for it.'

Which, it seemed, was going to be Derek's epitaph. Even in love, Jennet realised her man was not anything less than uncompromising and tough.

'Darling,' he murmured, 'you've got commitments in Australia, haven't you?'

'Yes.' She told him what they were, a television serial, a short season of one of Ibsen's plays.

'You'll have to honour them.'

'I'm afraid so.'

He sighed as he pulled himself up on to the pillows and turned her so that she lay with her face against his throat.

'Very well then,' he said. 'We'll have to get Derek's funeral over and it would be cruel to Melly to marry immediately. How the hell am I going to wait?' His voice roughened. His mouth found her ear and he began to whisper his need and desire. Words she had never hoped to hear, soft blunt words which excited her beyond belief so that her response was immediate and incandescent.

When next they lay at peace the cold grey light of dawn was trickling past the curtains.

'It will be good for our characters,' she told him sleepily, trying to raise her spirits. Then she spoilt it all by clinging desperately to him, burying her head in his shoulder. 'Oh, darling, darling, please take care. Don't go riding any horses and watch that damned truck doesn't explode again and be careful what you eat. I think I'll die away from you. I love you so. I love you so.'

'Hush,' he soothed, incredibly gentle, his hands trembling as they shaped her. 'My sweet lady, my soul's other keeper, don't cry. You be careful too. Watch out for maniac drivers and make sure nobody drops anything on to you from a skyscraper. And don't fall off the stage into the pit.'

'I promise.'

They kissed, slow, sweet, sleepy kisses to keep time at bay until they had to part, while outside every bird in the valley serenaded them.

After a while he asked urgently, 'Am I expecting too much of you? Can you be happy here, so far from any city? I couldn't bear it if you were unhappy. If you want to go on with your acting, we'll come to some sort of arrangement.'

If she had questioned the depth of his love, this effectively would have silenced her. That her uncompromising, ruthless Rafe should be prepared to surrender his primitive desire to be the centre of his woman's life, filled her with joy.

Pressing a kiss on to his chin she said, 'No, oh no. Acting has always been a stop-gap for me. I enjoy it and I'm quite good at it, but—does Port Arthur still run a good amateur dramatic society?'

'Yes.'

'Well then, I'll offer to help there. My real desire has always been to pot seriously. I'm better than quite good at that, and I'll improve. The owner of the craft shop at the Port told me that there are deposits of the right clay not too far away, and I'll have fun experimenting with glazes.'

She lifted her head to stare into the features which had always been so austere; the tender, amused adoration she saw there led to an alarming increase in her pulse rate.

'I suppose you'll want me to build you a kiln,' he teased, catching her chin with his finger.

'Please.'

He grinned and bent his head and kissed her, tracing the line of her mouth with the tip of his tongue. 'I can see that I'm not going to be able to resist you.'

'You don't have to any longer.'

'No, thank God. Darling, you don't know how good it is to feel you here, where you belong, after all these years. I should have recognised my fate when you were sixteen. It would have saved a lot of pain and misery all round.'

She shook her head. 'No, it wouldn't have worked. Nobody is ready for marriage so young. I would have bored you when you'd become used to having me in your bed. It's better this way.'

'It's certainly worth waiting for,' he said, making her blush with the narrowed intensity of his gaze, and the whispered love words that accompanied it, until at last it was time for them to leave the bed where their love had been consummated.

They were married on a glorious spring day in the small church in the valley where Hollingworths had prayed for generations.

Jennet wore pink the exact colour of the shadows in her hair, a soft, gently draped dress which revealed the slender elegance of her form while it gave her a little extra height. The colour and cut of the dress emphasised her striking beauty, but softened the potent allure that had been her despair. Melly, tall and slender in a deeper shade of pink, attended her. Derek's betrayal and death had left her numb, but she was fast recovering her normal spirits and she had asked to be Jennet's bridesmaid. Trent Addison was overseas, but letters arrived from him frequently and were answered with despatch.

At the altar, Jennet lifted adoring eyes to her tall, grave husband, met the leaping brilliance of his regard with a happiness which neither Derek's death nor Diana's presence could diminish.

Afterwards, in the hotel in Auckland where they spent that first night, before flying out to a friend's house on a tropical island in Fiji, they came together in a fire-storm of passion, all restraints gone.

'I'm sorry,' Rafe murmured huskily, when at last they lay quietly in each other's arms. His mouth touched the still heated skin where he had hurt her. 'I'm so sorry, my heart. It won't happen again, I promise, I swear.'

'I enjoyed it.' Jennet stretched like a sleepy cat, all temptress, her green eyes gleaming with lazy promise. 'And you bear a few marks, too. I like to watch you lose control and know that it's all my doing. Perhaps there's a little of Diana in me after all.'

He laughed. 'Gives you a sensation of power, does it?'

She had made a mistake mentioning her mother, though. Rafe's lashes hid the expression in his eyes but she sensed his withdrawal. He could not have forbidden Diana to attend her daughter's wedding, but it had angered him to watch her, still beautiful, still potently glamorous, dazzle the guests as she carried out the duties of a hostess with her usual confident *élan*.

Now Jennet's heart swelled as Rafe left the bed to

walk across to where champagne waited. Even in her mood of relaxed fulfilment, she felt a singing in her blood at the sight of him, so superbly balanced, his wide, smoothly muscled shoulders set above the tapering wedge of his body, the proud black head, the glowing, dark gold skin.

He was hers, and he loved her and she would die for him. Ghosts from the past could not be allowed to shadow their life together.

'I'm sorry I mentioned her,' she began, accepting the chilled, faintly golden wine. 'I'm sorry that she spoiled the wedding for you.'

He shrugged. 'Nothing could spoil the day I finally made you mine,' he said. 'Diana means nothing, is nothing, not now.'

Watching him over the rim of the glass, Jennet accepted that he was speaking the truth. Until that moment she had not realised how tense she had been. Now she sipped the cold, exquisite wine and felt her body relax into the pillows.

'Except that she's the mother of a very dear sister,' he said teasingly, 'and of the wife I love with all my heart. I should thank her. One day perhaps I will.'

'She won't be particularly pleased,' Jennet said slowly.

There was a touch of ruthlessness in his narrowed glance. 'I don't know that I ever made it my object to please Diana,' he said, adding unexpectedly, 'cctually, things could have been much worse. It was my father's tragedy that he allowed his desire for her to dominate and control his life.'

He came over and sat down on the side of the bed, the chiselled bone structure of his face softening into tenderness as he bent and kissed the hollow between her breasts.

'It wasn't her fault that I fought so desperately against exactly the same thing happening to me,' he said. 'I despised my father for his weakness; by the time I was seventeen I'd vowed quite consciously never to put myself in any woman's power. When I got to be twenty-three I thought I had my life under control. No woman had ever come close to me, I owned Te Puriri, I was all set to lead a bachelor's life until I could find the right sort of woman to give me heirs. A woman who wouldn't expect too much.' He laughed in self-mockery. 'Then you came home and all my smug satisfaction vanished like frost in sunlight, and I could see history repeating itself. I don't suppose you'll ever have any idea of what it was like for me those holidays. It didn't help to realise that you were every bit as conscious of me.'

'You were about as approachable as a hungry lion,' she said smiling, yet tender, as she traced the autocratic line of his jaw with her forefinger.

'That's vaguely how I felt.' His hand captured hers and he held it palm against his mouth. 'With a super-human amount of control I managed to leave you alone until that last day, but when I saw you lying like a dryad in your little dell, it was more than flesh and blood could stand.'

'I wouldn't have known,' Jennet said wistfully. 'You seemed fully in control until——'

'Until I was stupid enough to touch you.' He put his champagne glass on the cabinet by the bed, lifted hers from her hand and set it down in the same place. Then he swung himself on to the bed, sliding his arm beneath her shoulders to turn her to face him. 'And you responded so sweetly, with such innocent ardour, that I almost took you. I had to get the hell out of there, run away like a schoolboy caught stealing apples.' He laughed beneath his breath, 'And I'll never know where I got the strength.'

'But you are strong,' she said with quiet gravity. 'Strong and kind and generous.'

'How you can be so blind ...' He groaned and lowered his head to rest his forehead against hers. 'I know I've been all sorts of——'

'Hush.' Her fingers pressed his lips into silence.

His mouth moved into a kiss. Very quietly he asked 'Why did you marry Derek?'

'Oh, I don't know.' She sighed, choosing her words with care. 'I suppose—he made it obvious that he wanted me. I wasn't happy at university and Diana— well she was all for it. I was a coward and I took the easy way out. I think I knew that I wasn't in love with him but I thought—I hoped that we'd be able to make something of it. I was too young and stupid.'

He nodded, staring into her eyes as if he was trying to see into her soul. In his black depths there was pain and self-contempt and anger.

'I drank myself to sleep the night of the wedding,' he said.

'What??'

He gave her a twisted caustic smile. 'Don't look so shocked. I know you think I'm perfect, but I've committed all the usual stupidities. That night, after the festivities I retired to my room with a bottle and used it to stop myself from thinking of you in his bed. I literally couldn't bear to stay sober. I wouldn't give you away because I couldn't. I wanted you so much and I hated myself and you for the effect you had on me. I was a coward, and because of it we both suffered.'

Memories raced through Jennet's mind, somehow cleansed of pain and degradation. She hugged him close, resting her cheek against the short crisp hairs of his chest; the tactile sensations swarmed her blood and made her catch her breath.

A little half smile touched her mouth as her ear picked up the rapid increase in the rate of his heart beat.

Aloud, in a voice that was a little too even he said, 'What made you run away, finally?'

'Trent, of course. He arrived unexpectedly one night, just after Derek had hit me. Derek covered up, but Trent had seen—and heard—enough to work out what was going on. He left the next morning as he'd said he was going to. Derek went off to a sale in Kaitaia and as soon as he'd gone Trent came back. He just made it impossible for me to stay. He took me to friends of his in Auckland, made me see his lawyer, just took over.' She looked up into a face suddenly carved in granite. 'I know you don't like him much, Rafe, but I think he probably saved my life.'

'I didn't like him because I was bitterly jealous. He must have wanted you.' He held her startled eyes with his own, in a menacing stare. 'Did you sleep with him, Jennet? As a token of gratitude?'

Her eyes widened at the latent violence. 'No. *No*, Rafe! And he didn't want me. He knew Derek. He said that even as a child he was given to bouts of violent behaviour, that no one could control. He was sorry for me. He didn't touch me.'

He closed his eyes before forcing her head back on to the pillows with a kiss of savage intensity. Her surrender was complete and slowly the kiss was transmuted into tenderness and love. When it was over he lifted his head and made a small sound, his eyes fixed on the softly swollen contours of her mouth.

'How the hell am I going to prevent this bloody jealousy? It's barbaric, humiliating, yet I have no way to control it. I disliked Trent because I thought he'd had you. That's why I broke up his romance with Melly, such as it was.'

'When you learn to trust me you won't be jealous,' she promised.

He laughed at that, a soft, breathy sound which barely made it audible and brought his hands up to frame her face with a curious, gentle fierceness.

'I love you so,' he whispered, and it was all there in

his expression. His love was a fierce emotion, a strong, compelling force, predatory, even hard, yet in the tremor of the hands that cupped her face there was a rare tenderness and a vulnerability only she would ever see.

'I love you,' she said quietly. 'I wish I could tell you in a hundred different ways, but words can't do it, can they?'

'I can think of another way,' He smiled as his mouth touched hers. 'It doesn't involve much talking, but it gets the message across.'

Jennet felt his body harden, quicken against her, and the swift fire of her own response. Her mind visualised his face as it would be twenty years, forty years from then, and she knew with a great leap of the heart that whenever he looked at her it would always be with love, stronger than passion for all its strength, sweeter than tenderness for all its sweetness, rooted in both yet transcending them.

This, her heart told her, this is our world, and it is ours forever.

Harlequin *Presents*

Coming Next Month

Six exciting series
for you every month...
from Harlequin

Harlequin Romance·
The series that started it all

Tender, captivating and heartwarming...
love stories that sweep you off to faraway places
and delight you with the magic of love.

Harlequin Presents·
Powerful contemporary love
stories...as individual as the
women who read them

The No. 1 romance series...
exciting love stories for you, the woman of today...
a rare blend of passion and dramatic realism.

Harlequin Superromance®
It's more than romance...
it's Harlequin Superromance

A sophisticated, contemporary romance-fiction
series, providing you with a longer,
more involving read...a richer mix of complex plots,
realism and adventure.

Harlequin American Romance™
Harlequin celebrates the American woman...

...by offering you romance stories written about American women, by American women for American women. This series offers you contemporary romances uniquely North American in flavor and appeal.

◆

Harlequin Temptation
Passionate stories for today's woman

An exciting series of sensual, mature stories of love...dilemmas, choices, resolutions... all contemporary issues dealt with in a true-to-life fashion by some of your favorite authors.

◆

Harlequin Intrigue
Because romance can be quite an adventure

Harlequin Intrigue, an innovative series that blends the romance you expect... with the unexpected. Each story has an added element of intrigue that provides a new twist to the Harlequin tradition of romance excellence.

Harlequin Books·

PROD-A-2

HARLEQUIN HISTORICAL

Explore love with Harlequin in the Middle Ages, the Renaissance, in the Regency, the Victorian and other eras.

Relive within these books the endless ages of romance, set against authentic historical backgrounds. Two new historical love stories published each month.